CU00766960

Jesse's Triumph

AMRA PAJALIĆ

MELBOURNE, AUSTRALIA

https://www.pishukinpress.com/

Copyright © 2023 by Amra Pajalić

First Published 2023

Pishukin Press

All rights reserved. This book is copyright. Apart from fair dealing for the purpose of private study, research, criticism or review, as permitted under the copyright act, no part may be reproduced by any process without written permission from author.

Cover design: Created using Canva elements

For content and trigger warnings please go to www.amrapajalic.com/themes

Pre-publication data is available from the National Library of Australia
trove.nla.gov.au

Paperback Edition: 9781922871367

Content Warnings

SCAN QR CODE

OR GO TO

www.amrapajalic.com/
themes.html

Chapter 1

I was walking down the corridor, fixating on the scene in my novel, when my protagonist was lost in the woods. The world around me was slightly hazy and out of focus. I knew I was in my high school corridor and saw the students milling at their lockers around me, but they were distant, ethereal, my body on autopilot as I floated in my make-believe world.

Ow! Pain in my shin and I fell forward, hitting the linoleum floor hard, my palms stinging and my knees burning. I looked up to find Joshua King standing above me. He attempted a concerned mask ruined by the smirk tilting his lips. 'Sorry mate, didn't see you there.' He offered his hand under the guise of helping me up.

I knew better and ignored his proffered hand, standing up and wiping my jeans. His mates guffawed behind him. My cheeks burnt. I knew my milky skin showed all my emotions and, when I got embarrassed and red-faced, my blue eyes looked watery, like I was on the verge of tears. Sarah, my sister, teased me. I had a tragic face, and as a child I'd used it to sucker many an adult out of sweets. As I got older, it was a liability, especially in the cut-throat atmosphere of St Albans High.

I collected my books off the floor and walked around King and his idiot posse, staring at the floor. My rage built as I walked away. I was so sick of King and his bullshit. My mind turned to another scene, one of death and carnage. I ran to my safe space on the ground level of the three-storey building—the library.

When I walked in, I saw Brian, my best friend, sitting at a table. I rushed over, dropping to my knees in front of his desk.

'Joshua King,' I said. 'I'm putting him on my hit list.' I took out my notebook and took Brian's pen.

A girl was sitting next to Brian. I glanced at her and saw she was reading my page upside down. Her face blanched when she saw the heading, *People to kill.*

'Why?' Brian asked.

'He tripped me in the hall,' I said.

Brian read the next Maths answer from his notebook, but the girl beside him was stiff and unresponsive.

'Sabiha, this is my best friend, Jesse,' Brian introduced me.

I looked at the girl, recognising her as the new student who had begun a few weeks ago. She looked between me and Brian, obviously struggling to understand how we were best friends. Brian's brown hair was slicked back perfectly, and he wore black pleated pants and a dazzlingly white crisp shirt. He looked like he was going to a job interview. I wore loose jeans and an even looser sweatshirt, and both had seen better days. I'd never cared about my appearance until I saw myself through her eyes.

'We're in Phys Ed together,' I said, then regretted it as I saw the moment she remembered me, wincing as she flash-backed to our last lesson.

When our teacher, Mr Robinson, left the gym to go to his office, all the boys in class played dodgeball with me as the target. I'd flinched, trying to catch the balls, but I didn't have a chance in hell with multiple players targeting only me. Everyone laughed as the balls connected and bruised. I knew I'd become red-faced and watery-eyed again as rage worked through me, giving the bullies more hilarity as they revelled in thinking they'd made me cry.

When Mr Robinson returned and saw the balls on the floor around me, he'd asked me what happened. Mr Rob and I had a deal. I'd told him I couldn't nark on the kids anymore. He'd tried to punish the bullies for their idiotic behaviour in the past, which only led to more of the same. When I said nothing, Mr Rob ordered me to put the balls away. When we began playing soccer, he subtly punished King and his crew by not giving them their favourite positions. Their team lost, and mine won. It was a minor victory as victories went, but it was enough.

I noticed the book she was holding, Tara Moss' book *Split*. 'That one's great.' I took the book.

'You've read it too?' Sabiha sounded surprised.

'I can read.' I threw the book on the table. Did she equate me with King and his neanderthal brethren, incapable of stringing together a legible thought?

She grabbed my hand. 'I haven't met many boys who read.'

Sabiha smiled at me and my heart lightened; her green eyes sparkled, and her golden hair framed her face. My heart sped up for another reason.

'I was just surprised to find someone who shared my passion,' she explained.

'Jesse's the book-lover,' Brian said. 'I just read what he tells me to.'

She let go of my hand, and I clenched it, still feeling her touch. To hide my emotions, I looked at my watch. 'I've got to stock up on my rations.'

Seeing Sabiha's confusion, Brian translated. 'He needs to get reading material for the weekend.'

I quickly stood and went to the stack, peering at Brian and Sabiha through the gap in the shelf. As she stood and bent over to pack up, my skin heated as I noticed how her camouflage cargo pants curved around her waist. She straightened, revealing her bare midriff and curved waist.

'How long have you two known each other?' Sabiha asked.

'Since primary school.' Brian put his Maths book away.

'Has he always wanted to kill people?'

'Jesse's not a weirdo or anything. He uses fantasy to deal with the bullying. He couldn't hurt anyone.'

'Good to know,' she said.

My stomach dropped. Of course, she thought I was dangerous. What kind of weirdo talked about killing people at a school? I gently hit my forehead on the books in front of me. Shit! I glanced around, checking if anyone could see me. I had to be more careful. People already thought I was weird. I didn't have to help them.

I quickly pulled a few books from the shelves, needing a comfort read, returning to my favourites of John Green and Melina Marchetta. Sabiha and Brian had packed up and were waiting by the counter.

I placed my books on the counter next to Sabiha. 'This is a new title,' Miss Swan, the librarian, said as she scanned the latest John Green book. 'Write a recommendation since you're the first lender.'

I smiled, excited by the thought. As a writer, any byline helped boost my confidence. I placed my books in my book-bag and caught sight of Sabiha's face. She was frowning as she eyed me and the librarian. I looked away. She hated me. What did I expect? I'd thought I had an ally. As if?

Brian and Sabiha walked ahead of me as we walked out of the library and up the stairs to the second storey. We had History together.

Sabiha followed Brian to the back of the class and threw her backpack on the table next to him. I hesitated next to her, meeting Brian's gaze. Usually, Brian and I sat at the back. I doodled on the edges of my notepad as the teacher spoke while Brian stared out the window, caught up in his own world. If the teacher called on Brian, I'd quickly jot down the answer he could read out, maintaining the impression that he was engaged in class.

'Let's move one down so Jesse can sit on the other side.' Brian waved to her right.

Sabiha looked at me, flushing slightly, as she moved one seat down. I sat in the chair next to the window. 'So altruistic of you to give up your favourite seat,' I murmured.

Brian shot me a frown but said nothing as he sat between us.

The teacher asked us to discuss whether World War I or World War II was the war that affected the world the most. Brian moved his seat back so that he included Sabiha, as no one was sitting next to her.

'World War I because it's the first war that involved the entire world,' Brian said.

'I agree because it's also the fact that it changed the class system. It brought about the demise of the aristocracy, and there were millions of deaths, both during the war and afterwards, from the Influenza,' I added.

'It might have been responsible for more deaths, but it was steeped in the traditions of trench warfare,' Sabiha said. 'The second world war was much more brutal and bloody because it was about genocide and extermination. Hitler's ideology has become a blueprint that keeps repeating. Just look at what's happening in my corner of the world.'

I frowned, not understanding what she was referring to.

'I'm Bosnian. Ethnic cleansing is a new term, but it's the same concept. Exterminate an entire race of people for a land grab.'

The penny dropped. It was years ago, but I'd seen news reports about the Balkan Conflict as the country that was once Yugoslavia tore itself apart, with each state seeking independence after their dictator Tito, who had ruled for forty years, died.

'Can you really compare the ethnic cleansing of Bosnia and the Holocaust, though?' I questioned, my intellectual brain engaged. Usually, Brian made a one-sentence announcement and then attempted to segue the conversation into his social life. This was the first time I'd actually had someone to debate.

Sabiha's jaw tightened. 'I wasn't comparing. I was justifying my argument that the second world war was more brutal.' She turned away, crossing her arms on her chest as she stared straight ahead at the whiteboard.

'Don't be a sore loser,' I stirred.

She looked at me, her green eyes flashing ire. 'I'm not,' she spat. 'To you, this is an intellectual discussion about war. To me, this is real life. My family were brutalised and chased out of their homeland. So excuse me if I don't want to trade details to win an argument.'

I flushed, looking down at the table as I scratched the edge. I'd been so engaged in the discussion I hadn't thought through that I was pushing emotional buttons. The teacher asked us to share, but our group remained stubbornly silent.

'Apologise,' Brian wrote on the edge of his notebook and held it to me. When I read it, he quickly scrawled over it and transformed it into a love heart.

Sabiha was frosty for the rest of the double, barely looking at me.

'I want to apologise,' I said as we packed up a few minutes before the bell. 'I didn't mean to be insensitive.'

'That's fine,' Sabiha snapped.

'Sabiha, Jesse apologised. Now you accept his apology,' Brian intervened.

She glared at him. Brian maintained eye contact. She wilted.

'I accept,' she muttered, swinging her backpack onto her back.

The bell rang, and we drifted out of the classroom and down the stairs.

'See you tomorrow.' Brian kissed her on the cheek at the bottom of the stairs. The boys' lockers were at the other end of the corridor.

She smiled, her face transformed. 'See you.'

'Jesse,' Brian prodded, looking at me.

'See you tomorrow,' I muttered, waving quickly.

Sabiha's smile faded. 'See you.'

I opened my locker, carefully checking my diary for all the homework and collecting the notebooks and textbooks I'd need. Brian emptied his backpack of textbooks and notebooks.

'Really!' I exclaimed.

'I don't need those when I've got you.' Brian smiled widely and put his arm around my shoulders. He came over every night after I'd finished my homework and used my notes and homework to complete his.

'Eventually, the teachers will figure out you're not doing any of your own work.' It surprised me it hadn't happened already. While Brian could complete the homework using me as a resource when we were doing the exams, he had to pass on his own, and somehow he always did.

'Please. They'll only figure it out if I over-reach. But I know my speed. I'm a bare-pass student.' He preened in front of the mirror he'd attached to the inside of his locker door, using his comb to slick back his dark hair.

'The fact that you pass all the exams means you've got a great memory. If you tried, you could get a great grade.'

'What do I need good grades for?' He slammed the locker shut as his face darkened. 'I know where my future is.'

I gently closed my locker door, not saying anything. Brian's father was an immovable boulder.

We walked home together. When we reached my house, Brian continued, waving as he called out, 'See you soon.'

I took my key from my pocket and unlocked the front door.

Mum was in the living room, sitting in her wheelchair in front of the TV. The bright colours of the TV show The Price is Right lit up her face in the darkened room, the sun setting early in winter.

I flicked on the light switch. Mum turned to look at me, a smile brightening her face.

'You shouldn't be sitting in the dark,' I chastised.

'Reggie, you're back from work,' she exclaimed, calling me by my father's name. He'd been dead since I was four years old, hit by a drunk driver, but lately, Mum sometimes confused me for him. I hardly had any memories of him. Just a vague impression of a show, maybe Moomba, as there was a river and water-skiers. I couldn't see, so he lifted me on his shoulders. He towered above the other partygoers at six foot four, and I'd reached my hands up, convinced I could touch the sky.

Sometimes when I looked at the scant photo album charting my life with him, the ten photos of just me and him, I had a glimpse of a memory, a shimmer that quickly faded. My fourth birthday and the car birthday cake Mum made. Him lighting the candles, urging me to blow them, feeling his breath next to my ear as he helped me blow. I'd examined myself in the mirror, trying to see the resemblance. Something in the way the stubble covered my skin highlighted my square chin and high cheekbones. The one thing I'd wanted from him was his towering height, but alas, my mother's genes had dominated, and I was only 5 foot 10.

Mum's face cleared as she recognised me. 'Jesse, tell me about your day,' she demanded.

I placed my backpack on the shoe shelf in the hallway and wheeled her to the kitchen. 'First up, I had English,' I told her, as I opened the fridge and took out carrots, celery, capsicum, and the eggplant dip that was her favourite. 'We had a class debate about the ethics of cloning for language analysis.' I closed the fridge and took out the chopping board. 'My team won, of course.' I chopped the vegetables and placed them on a platter, fanning them out around the eggplant as I told her the Disney version of my day. There was a debate, but Joshua King was in my English class and made it a point to torment me by interrupting me every time I spoke. The teacher attempted to stop Joshua at the beginning of the year, but now was completely worn down and just let the class bully suck all the attention from the room.

I pushed Mum's wheelchair to the kitchen table and sat across from her. As we ate our snacks, she laughed at my jokes, her full cheeks wobbling.

'I love you, Jesse,' Mum said, her hand patting mine.

I held her hand in mine. Her fingers were thick and swollen, her knuckles barely visible. She'd had breast cancer five years ago and, as part of her treatment, had her lymph nodes removed, which affected her thyroid. At first, the doctors thought she suffered from depression. She was tired and slept most of the day, and her short-term memory deteriorated. She attempted to keep up with her job as a nurse but cut back her hours more and more as fatigue hit her. Her memory began failing, and she made a few mistakes on the job. She was put on sick leave. Without a job, she drifted increasingly into lethargy, sleeping all day, gaining more and more weight. By the time she was diagnosed with hypothyroidism a year later, her career was in ruins, and she was morbidly obese and struggling to function.

I wheeled Mum back to the living room and parked the chair in front of the TV. She smiled as I turned the television screen back on. I returned to the kitchen, washed the dishes, and then checked the casserole I had started in the slow cooker this morning. I put on the rice in the rice cooker, glancing at the clock. I had an hour and a half until my sister Sarah returned from work. I went to my bedroom. I turned on my computer, flicking through my notes and working on my English homework. When I finished, I went to the backyard with a washing basket, collecting the washing from the clothesline I'd put up in the morning. I folded it as I went, returning to the house and placing the dried clothes in our wardrobes and drawers.

I checked on the rice cooker and the slow cooker. Both were finished and on warming. I served the table, putting out three dinner plates and cups, and the cutlery, then returned to my bedroom and started my history homework. I heard the front door open, and Sarah called out. Her murmurs from the front room as she kissed Mum hello, followed by footsteps down the hall and a quick knock on my door before she peered in. 'Hello, baby bro.' She blew a kiss.

I smiled at her. She looked so much like me. The same blonde hair and blue eyes, the shape of the face. We both took after Mum. Looking at Sarah was like looking at Mum twenty years ago. Sometimes it made me sad. If Mum had been diagnosed earlier, how different would our lives have been?

'See you in ten.' Sarah went to her bedroom, and I heard the shower.

It was the first thing she did when she came home, jump in the shower and get rid of all the clothes she wore. Nursing was grimy work, and she felt she had to decontaminate hers. Sarah was twenty-two, six years older than me. After Mum went into remission, we expected life would return to normal, but it didn't. The thyroid medication that she used wasn't effective and had some pretty nasty side-effects.

Those were tough years. We survived on a pension Mum received from the government. We had to go to the food bank, and all my clothes were secondhand and frayed. Our extended family had to chip in regularly to help with large bills, and every time there was a visit from the Department of Human Services, our Aunt Cara came to stay overnight, pretending that she was living with us, to fend them away. When Sarah turned eighteen, she did a nursing course and started working full-time. At least the financial struggle eased a bit, but I had to take on more household duties to relieve the burden from her. I didn't mind. I was just relieved that those days of stress and scarcity were behind us.

While Sarah was showering, I served up the food and placed it on the table. Mum wheeled herself from the kitchen. As I brought over a jug of water, Sarah walked in, wearing grey tracksuit pants and a matching top, her hair tied up loosely in a ponytail.

'You're a lifesaver.' She sat down and lifted the serving ladle. 'I didn't have time to take a lunch break.' She heaped her platter and began eating, shovelling in four spoonfuls by the time I had served Mum and me.

'That's better,' Sarah said after a few more spoonfuls. 'My stomach has stopped attempting to eat itself. How was your day? Anything interesting happen?'

'We had a class debate.' I sipped water.

'You did. How did you go?' Mum asked me. She had forgotten. Even though I'd told her the story two hours before. Another side effect of her condition.

I told the story again, this time for Sarah's benefit. We always began with my day. Sarah could only tell her work stories when we weren't eating, as most of the ones she found interesting or funny involved bodily fluids.

'Oh, also I met the new girl,' I added, serving myself another portion.

'New girl?' Sarah's spoon paused on its way to her mouth. 'Name, description, attributes?'

'Sabiha, blonde, blue-eyed, Bosnian Muslim. And I guess her key attribute was angry.'

'So she's the angry new girl?' Sarah smiled as she spoke.

'I guess she has reason to be. She's Bosnian Muslim, and her family came from the war.'

'Mmm. You forgot to mention she's pretty.' A wicked smile lit up Sarah's face.

'What? I don't need to say that.' Even as I was speaking, I felt my cheeks flushing. I had been awestruck the first time I saw her, and as we argued in history, I had felt more than the stirrings of intellectual debate.

'Oooh, so she's really pretty,' Sarah prodded.

My cheeks got hotter, and I flashed her an angry look.

'Stop teasing your brother,' Mum intervened. 'Just because Jesse finds the new girl pretty doesn't mean we have to tease him.'

'Muuuum,' I wailed.

Sarah and Mum chuckled. This was the problem with being the only male in the house. I was constantly outnumbered and outmanoeuvred.

'What was your day like?' I asked Sarah, desperately hoping for a tale of horrible bodily fluids to take the attention of me.

'Oh, have I got a story for you.' Sarah cracked her knuckles, a gleeful look on her face. She loved telling excruciating stories. 'A man came in. Or should I say, hobbled in. After he'd checked in, claiming an excruciating stomach ache, he wouldn't sit down.'

I closed my eyes and shuddered. It was going to be one of those excruciating stories about an obstruction in the bowel. Sarah gestured and mimed as she revealed details of the interview and investigation. When she shared details of the extraction, I had to breathe through my gag reflex. This was the problem with getting your wish. It was always a regret.

After we ate, I collected the dishes.

'Shoo.' Sarah took the plate off me and shooed me. 'I'll do the dishes.'

'It's okay. I've got time.'

'You've done enough for today.' Sarah went to the kitchen and filled the dishwasher while I returned to my bedroom. Sarah still had to bathe mother before bed, but she always wanted to be fair.

As I was completing my Maths homework, there was a brief knock, and the door opened. I knew without looking it was Brian. He had a distinctive knock of refusing to wait for the all-clear before barging in.

He threw himself on my bed and sighed. I spun in my chair and turned to him. 'Do you want to talk about it?'

He was lying on my bed with his hand over his face. He shook his head. 'No point.'

I turned back and left him. He must have had another argument with his father. Nothing else laid him as low.

'Okay, I'm ready.' He sat up.

I handed him my notebooks. He scrawled on sheets of paper. I finished my homework and flicked to the document where my mate, Charlie, and I were working on a graphic novel. Charlie was autistic, and while he was high functioning and so could endure the hallways of a public high school, he had found ways to cope. One of them was wearing headphones every day.

Another was fictionalising the school into a post-apocalypse world where everyone was a zombie or survivor. We'd started the project as a lark in our graphic design class when we were paired up, mostly because we were the class rejects.

At first, Charlie hadn't wanted to speak to me at all, but I'd watched him with his sketchbook. I began writing captions for his drawings that I showed him. He loved it, and pretty soon we were collaborating. One day, he showed me a blank page. He wanted me to write the story, and he would draw it. And so that's how we started. Now it has become a therapeutic after-school activity. I would write about what happened to me during the day, but re-setting it into my imaginary world and email it to Charlie. He'd send me the images the next day.

Charlie drew in black and white pencil and then scanned it. He got a fancy scanner that his extended family had pooled money for his last Christmas present, wanting to give him a chance for self-expression.

After I received the new pages, I'd lay them out using the publishing software we had access to at school. We impressed our graphic design teacher with our progress and story. Somehow he hadn't twigged that all the zombies were based on my classmates.

I looked at Charlie's photos and laughed as I saw Joshua King's zombie clone being killed with a hammer pounded to the head. I heard Brian shifting on my bed behind me. He stood and leaned over my shoulder.

'How many times have you killed Joshua King now?' he scoffed.

'Not enough,' I muttered as I saved the images to my computer.

'Listen,' Brian cleared his throat. 'About what happened in the library today—'

'I know,' I interrupted him. 'I completely freaked Sabiha out.'

'Yeah. She doesn't really know you yet. So we should probably keep all this on the down-low from her.'

I looked at the images before me. I was so used to them that the gruesomeness didn't register. There were images of body parts being hacked off, hands twitching as zombies were dismembered and blood, guts and gore spilling out in a multitude of ways.

'Yep, you're right.' I vowed not to mention anything to Sabiha, then I paused. 'Hang on, so she's going to be a regular girl hang?' I looked over my shoulder at him. Brian had gravitated towards girls as friends, but usually these were short-term goss sessions that didn't last longer than a few days. This was the first time he'd expressed interested in a girl.

'Yeah, she's special,' Brian smiled. 'I want her to stick around.'

I nearly said, I thought you were into guys, but bit back my words just in time. Brian had never officially come out, and I'd never asked. 'This is the first time you've had a crush,' I said instead.

'Maybe I just hadn't met the right girl,'

'Yeah, maybe you're right?' I turned around, a stone sinking in my stomach. Why did I care Brian liked Sabiha? 'I'm happy for you, man,' I forced out past my lips.

'Thanks bud. I knew I could count on you.' Brian patted my shoulder and headed for the door. 'Tomorrow.'

After he left, I turned back to my graphic novel. At least this was one constant.

Chapter 2

Brian and I walked to school together in the morning. 'There she is,' Brian waved enthusiastically. Sabiha waved back. She was wearing a denim skirt and chunky boots, her legs—lean and long—a Metallica t-shirt stretched across her torso. I'd made an effort, wearing my newest baggy sweatshirt and jeans, while Brian was in his black pleated pants and a blue silk shirt.

When we approached, he and Sabiha kissed each other on the cheek. Sabiha turned toward me and leaned in. I stepped back shyly.

Her face creased in displeasure, and she turned back to Brian. 'How was your weekend?' she demanded, hooking her arm through Brian's.

The two of them walked ahead of me, and I watched them flirting. Brian was doing his trademark PDA, effortlessly curving his hand around Sabiha's waist. It pissed me off how comfortable he was with the opposite sex. He had no problems talking to girls or flirting. I wished I could be as natural as he was, instead, I turned into a stiff tin man.

We sat in our usual seating at the back, Brian in the middle during Maths. The two of them giggled and sent each other notes while the teacher had his back turned. I copied from the whiteboard, pressing hard into the paper with my pen. One of us had to do some actual school work.

'I completely flaked and didn't take down any notes.' Sabiha giggled at the end of the lesson.

'That's okay. I'll copy Jesse's tonight, and then you can get them off me.' Brian put his arm around my shoulders.

'Or maybe the two of you can actually concentrate in class and do your work.' I shrugged off his arm irritably.

'What would be the fun in that?' Brian chided.

'Yeah, that's why we have you.' Sabiha followed from the classroom.

I stewed. I was just their glorified note-taker.

'Laters.' Brian hugged Sabiha before going off to home economics. He'd refused to take PE and had gotten a note from his doctor that he had an injury to avoid it.

I looked at Sabiha awkwardly. 'PE,' I stated the obvious and walked to the gym. I realised I was walking ahead of her and slowed, so she caught up with me.

I tried to remember the me who was optimistic at the beginning of the year when I thought PE was a good idea. My plan was to get fit, chase off the last of my pre-adolescent puppy fat, and thought it would help. I hadn't accounted for the psycho, Joshua King.

Sabiha and I lined up with our class in front of the gym doors. I tried to think of something to say, a conversation starter, but my tongue was tied.

'I hope it's not netball today,' Sabiha moaned. 'I'm so sick of it.'

'Yeah, me too.' I lied. I actually loved netball. It didn't give Joshua the opportunity to torment me because we had the net to separate us.

We split up and went into our change rooms. I went to the corner that I'd marked as my own. As I changed, I kept my back to the wall and my eyes on the changing room. I'd learnt to wear my sports shorts and t-shirt beneath my clothes so I didn't have to actually change, so much as strip off. I never knew when Joshua was going to strike.

I jogged out. Sabiha was on the gym floor, her black shorts revealing her long legs, her t-shirt fitted and showing off her waist. I felt my breath catch as I caught sight of her. She saw me and smiled, waving me over.

'We're playing basketball.' She scrunched up her nose, looking adorable. 'My only goal is to stay the hell away from the ball. Be my defence.' She yanked me in front of her. My biceps tingled at her touch.

As usual, Joshua King was one captain and George Georgiou was the other. Each of them began with their mates. After his mates surrounded him like a posse, Joshua gave Sabiha the once-over. 'New girl.' He pointed at her.

George looked disappointed.

'You snooze, you lose.' Joshua smirked at George, looking like the king of the hill.

'No.' Sabiha crossed her arms over her chest. 'Let's make it easy. Whoever knows my name gets to pick me.' She waited.

'My girl, Sabiha,' George said with a smile.

'My man, George.' Sabiha approached him and gave him a high five.

Joshua's smirk faded, and he frowned at her. 'Hey, it's my turn!'

'Not today. Today it's this lady's turn.' She turned back toward me. 'And Jesse has to come with. He's my defence.' She yanked me by the arm, so I joined George's team.

'That's not fair. You can't take my turn and then pick someone else,' Joshua huffed.

'Go cry about it to Mr Robinson. See if he gives a shit.' Sabiha marched on, pulling me with her.

As usual, Mr Robinson was sitting on the bench at the back of the gym, staring at a folder on his lap. He had the Athletics carnival to organise, and the past few weeks left the class to their devices as he used class time to coordinate it.

Joshua's stare hardened as he looked at Sabiha. Shit, he was going to get revenge.

'You shouldn't have done that,' I told her as we waited for the picking to finish. 'Joshua's going to come at you.'

'Bigger and better than him have tried and failed.' Sabiha looked at me cockily.

Anger churned in my stomach. Didn't she know how to stay under the radar? Everywhere she went, trouble followed, and now I was paired up with her and would be in the firing line.

She was watching Joshua with a gleam in her eye. She thought this was a game. Shit, I would have to protect her from herself. This was my chance to stand up to Joshua and not let him get away with his shit.

The game started, and I followed the ball. Sabiha stuck close to me, but then we got separated by a melee. Joshua got the ball and headed toward Sabiha, dribbling, his eyes laser beam focused. I could see the thought as he went for her. He would slam into her hard, sending her sprawling onto the hardwood floor. It was a trick he'd performed many a time on me.

I ran, to head him off, but his mates surrounded me. Joshua was approaching Sabiha. Shit, he was going to hit her! Someone blocked me, and I couldn't see. I heard a thud, a scream echoing around the gym. The action stopped. I pushed Anton out of the way and ran to Sabiha. She was on the ground, her legs sprawled, tears in her eyes. Joshua stood above her, his face formed into an 'oh' of surprise.

'What did you do, you prick!' I slammed my hands into his chest, making him drop the ball as he stepped back.

'I didn't touch her!' he shouted.

'Lying scum.' I slammed him again.

Mr Robinson threw himself in between us. 'That's enough, Jesse. Joshua, go to the principal's office. I'll come deal with you.'

'I didn't touch her,' Joshua shouted.

'Now!' Mr Robinson roared, pointing his arm toward the gym doors.

Joshua looked at his mates helplessly before spinning on his heel and leaving.

I ran to Sabiha's side and knelt beside her. 'Are you okay?'

She nodded, wiping a tear. I took her arm and helped her up. She winced in pain.

'Take her to first aid, Jesse,' Mr Robinson said.

I slowly led Sabiha from the gym. She hobbled, leaning against me. When we were out of the gym and had turned left, she straightened and walked normally.

'And that's how it's done.' She pushed her hair over her shoulder and looked at me with a shit-eating grin.

I stopped in surprise. 'You were faking!'

'Shhh.' She put her finger on my lips and led me away from the gym doors. 'We don't want Mr Robinson to know. I wonder if we can get an icy from the canteen. I mean, I am a patient and all.' She headed toward the canteen. 'Are you coming?'

I ran to catch up to her. 'Aren't you scared Mr Robinson will follow up with the nurse?'

'Nah. We'll come back near the end of the lesson, and I'll tell him I waited until the icepack took effect. He's not the sort of teacher who asks too many questions.'

I was too stunned to speak. When we got to the canteen, she put on a plaintive face. 'We're just in PE, and I took quite a tumble. I cut my mouth and was hoping I could buy an icy to soothe it.' She covered her mouth and winced.

'Of course, dearie.' The canteen lady slid open the freezer.

'Actually, can I get two? I'll use one for my knee,' Sabiha added.

The woman nodded and slid them across the counter. Sabiha rifled in her bra and produced a note.

We went out and sat at the tables in front of the canteen. 'Here.' She held out the second icy.

'What about your knee?' I teased as I sat across from her.

'I thought you could lick it after you eat your icy,' she said, her face serious.

My eyes widened, and I jerked back.

'Just kidding.' She chortled with laughter, nearly falling backwards off the bench.

I grabbed her hand and yanked her forward, holding her hand a little too long.

'Thanks buddy,' she said.

We sat in silence, licking the icy. This was the best PE lesson I'd ever had. It was a lovely warm day, and we were in the shade. Still, I couldn't rest easy.

'Aren't you afraid of Joshua King? He's going to want to get revenge.'

'He's just a thug. You just have to put him in his place.' She sucked out the juice in the bottom of her plastic tube. 'Anyway, I've got you to protect me.'

I looked at her with surprise.

'After the way you went at him, he'll think twice before coming after me.'

I rewound the action in my mind, replaying the moment I'd pushed him and his stunned face as he nearly fell. I'd been fearless, only concerned with Sabiha's welfare. I'd never stood up to Joshua like that before. When he'd picked on me before, I'd just taken it as if it was all I deserved. My back straightened. Having Sabiha look at me as someone who could be her protector changed something in me. Maybe she saw something I didn't.

'You're right. I'll fuck him up if he tries messing with you.' I mimicked the words I'd heard other boys in the schoolyard say to each other, testing the way they came out of my mouth.

'My hero.' Sabiha put her head on my shoulder and patted me.

I inspected her face. Was she being sarcastic? She held my gaze, completely sincere. My stomach fluttered, and my eyes moved to her lips, the urge to kiss her overwhelming me. She leaned forward. Was she going to kiss me? It was going to happen.

Her lips brushed my cheek. 'I'm so glad I've got you and Brian to have my back.'

She took the plastic tube from my hand and got up, tossing both in the rubbish bin. I remained seated, still frozen. My mind caught in the almost kiss.

'We'd better get back.'

I stood, and she leaned back against me as she fake-hobbled her way into the gym. When we entered, Mr Robinson came over. 'Any better.'

'Just a bit sore,' Sabiha said.

I peered at the benches. Joshua was nowhere to be seen.

'I'll make sure that doesn't happen again on my watch,' Mr Robinson said.

I sat with Sabiha on the bench and watched the game. Mr Robinson was actively supervising.

'I'm guessing he doesn't want me to complain that I was hurt because he wasn't supervising,' Sabiha said wryly.

'But you weren't hurt.' I was stung on Mr Robinson's behalf. He was a good teacher and took care of me.

'Only because of my quick thinking. What do you think would have happened if Joshua caught up with me?'

I flashed back to the rage on Joshua's face as he'd dribbled toward Sabiha. I'd been terrified, knowing he wouldn't pull his punches and elbow her hard. I'd been many a recipient of his faux defence and had ended up with bruises on my ribs. Sabiha was much smaller and slighter than me. She could have even ended up with a broken bone. I vowed I would not let her be in danger again. She thought I was her protector and I would fulfil that role.

Mr Robinson whistled for the game to end, and we went to the change room. I helped Sabiha hobble to the changing room, enjoying my last few minutes of physical contact. Being in the changing room without Joshua's menacing presence was a relief. After I changed, I jogged out and approached Mr Robinson.

'How do I sign up for the weights' room?' I asked.

Mr Robinson looked at me with surprise. There was a weights room next to the school gym that students signup to, either before or after school. I'd watched the muscle-bound boys going in and out, feeling intimidated by their tough physique, the macho way they walked, as if they had five kilogram balls they dragged on the ground.

'We're full.' Mr Robinson said.

My face dropped with disappointment.

'Actually, let me check.' He got the signup folder and came to me. He opened the folder, and there was a list of boys—all the muscle heads. Mr Robinson crossed out Joshua King's name, and Anton's below him. 'A spot just opened up.' He wrote my name down.

'Thanks.'

'Nothing to thank me for. Joshua has to face consequences for his actions today. And Anton was argumentative afterwards, so he needs to know too.'

I walked away, feeling guilty. Anton was probably just trying to tell Mr Robinson the truth that Sabiha had faked the dive. It didn't seem fair that he would lose out on the weights room too, but then again, Sabiha was right. If she hadn't been so quick thinking and dropped to the ground, she would have been badly injured, and Anton hadn't intervened to stop his best friend. I straightened my shoulders. I needed to toughen up like Sabiha. They both got what was coming to them.

***

After school, I met Brian at the lockers. 'I'm staying back because I signup up for the weights' room.' I'd called our neighbour Mrs O'Malley and asked her to check in with Mum, as I was going to be an hour late home.

'Really. That's awesome.' Brian punched me in the arm. 'I wish I signed up too.'

I don't know what reaction I'd expected, but this wasn't it. Since starting high school, Brian had avoided sports and physical exertion like the plague. I thought it was in rebellion against his father's expectations that he was a macho man. In primary school, he'd been on the soccer team and was a fierce player, but he'd never gone to the oval since coming to high school. I'd never asked why. I'd just assumed he didn't want to be associated with the meatheads, like me.

'Actually, you can.' I gave him the lowdown about what happened in PE and about Anton and Joshua being scrubbed out of the weights room.

'Wow, so you actually stood up to that lug-head.'

I nodded, a smile on my lips. I was pretty pleased with myself.

'Sabiha really is something. I don't think I've ever met a girl like her.' Admiration coloured his voice.

'Yep.' I twisted away. I couldn't covet by best friend's girlfriend. Even though Sabiha and Brian weren't official, he'd staked his claim first.

'Let's go get ripped.' Brian ruffled my hair as we walked down the stairs and to the gym. Brian sniffed audibly as we entered the weights room. 'Oh, the musty perfume of sweaty adolescent male.'

A few boys were already there, and they glanced at the two of us curiously. 'Cut it out,' I muttered under my breath.

Brian always used humour when he was uncomfortable, which only drew more attention to the situation.

We made our way around the weights. We got to the deadlift, and Brian went first, lifting thirty kilograms in ten reps. I went after him and was wilting after six. How was he able to do so much more? He was much more wiry than me.

'All that bricklaying is paying off.' Brian smirked as he did a biceps curl and showed off his taut biceps.

I snapped my towel at him, and he laughed.

By the end of the hour, I was sweaty and sore. As we headed out, I walked slowly, my muscles feeling the burn.

'We're going to be buff like all the macho lug-heads in no time.' Brian postured as he walked.

I laughed with him. 'How come you stopped playing soccer?'

Brian's smile faded. 'Other boys don't like it when you're too different. My fashion consciousness was just a little too on the nose for them.' Brian tapped his nose.

I knew what he was saying. I'd heard others mention rumours about him being gay. He was obviously different from the other boys in our year level: he always styled his hair, and loved experimenting with his look. I'd realised that he sometimes wore foundation after I'd seen it in his bedroom. He'd said he took it from his mother and wore it to cover up pimples. That's why our friendship worked. We were both outliers to our peers. I never fitted in with the lug-heads either. I had to grow up too soon and do housework around the house when so many of my male peers only undertook the stereotypical 'male' chores.

'It's a shame you gave up something you loved for those losers. We need to stop letting others define us and let them set our limitations.' I'd let Joshua bully me for so long because I'd just perceived a pecking order and that I was at the bottom. It had never even occurred to me to stand up to him until Sabiha came on the scene.

'You're right,' Brian mused. 'I let the fuckers win.'

'Just like I let Joshua win. I'm never going to be that asshole's punching bag again.' I fisted my hands.

'Are you sure about that?' Brian looked at me askance.

'Yep. Definitely sure.' I snapped.

'Then turn around.'

Brian was looking behind me. I spun around, dread settling in my stomach. Sure enough, Joshua and Anton loomed toward us. The bastards must have been lying in wait.

'James, you prick,' Joshua shouted as he got closer. 'You stole my place in the weights' room.'

I stood my ground as he thrust his face into mine. 'No, I didn't. Mr Robinson scratched you off to punish you.'

'But I did nothing!' Joshua shouted.

'Yeah, he was set up,' Anton chimed in.

'You did nothing this time. And that's only because Sabiha fell before you got to her. If she didn't, she'd be in hospital.' I spoke without heat, not wanting to inflame the situation further.

'Please, I was just going to give her a love tap.' Joshua brushed off my words with a wave of his hand.

'Really.' I lifted my top and showed the bruises discolouring my torso. 'Like this love tap? What do you think would have happened to a girl half your size if you hit into her like you did with me?'

Joshua looked at my bruises in shock.

'Shit, brah, you really did some damage,' Anton blanched and stepped away.

'Yes, he did. Every week.' I put my t-shirt down. 'But you will never do it again. You come at me again, anywhere, anytime, and I'll put you in your place. And if you try to touch Sabiha, I'll put you in the ground.' This time I didn't remain calm. My voice was full of fury and heat.

'And I'll fucking knock your block off if you touch either of my mates.' Brian stepped into the fray, fists waving wildly.

King hesitated, debating whether he was going to back down. He cut his eyes toward Anton, checking to see if his brah was on his side. Anton was looking at Joshua with caution, finally understanding the consequences of what would have happened if he'd hit Sabiha.

'I've got to get home.' Anton stepped away, signalling he wasn't backing Joshua in this fray.

King stepped away, raising his hands in surrender, a coward who would only biffo if he had the numbers on his side. 'Fine. You stay out of my way, I'll stay out of yours.'

'With pleasure.' I dead-eyed him.

Joshua broke eye contact first, stepping away to join Anton. Joshua gesticulated in anger as they walked away, while Anton determinedly strode away.

'Shit, we actually did it. We stood up to the lug-heads, and we're still standing.' I folded my arms behind my head as I walked in circles, adrenaline and fatigue battling within my body.

'Yep. We fucking are.' Brian hugged me and started jumping. 'You've inspired me. I'm going to play soccer again.'

'Good.' I walked straighter on my weary legs. I didn't know when this day started who I was going to become. That I would become the guy who stood up to Joshua King, my tormenter for years. Who knew who I would become tomorrow?

***

Chapter 3

I was sitting on the bench at the front of our school. Brian and Sabiha were on the bench across from me, her arm hooked in his, her leg across his. Seeing them becoming closer in the past week had been both painful and joyful.

Dina and Gemma approached. I had classes with both of them this year, but we'd never spoken. They stood next to Sabiha, but she purposely ignored them.

Dina bent down and scrutinised Brian's face, her brown hair swinging by her face like a curtain while her gold necklace dangled in the air. 'You're wearing foundation,' she burst out in a shrill voice.

'It's Clearasil,' Brian said without skipping a beat.

I didn't know what to say. I knew Brian wore foundation and found Dina's obnoxious way of putting him down irritating, but what could I say?

We examined his face. A layer of orange cream concealing the large pimples on his cheeks and chin.

'Looks like foundation to me,' Gemma said, a sly smile as she twirled a lacklustre red-curl from her home-perm.

Sabiha stood and stared them down. 'Why aren't you on the oval?' she demanded, making a shooing gesture.

Dina's lips tightened, and then she forced a smile. 'Do you want to join us?'

'Sure,' Brian jumped in before Sabiha could speak, pulling her up by the arm.

Brian and I walked behind the girls as we walked to the oval. Gemma and Dina had taken a position on each side of Sabiha and whispered in her ear.

'Since when do you want to hang around the Evil Vortex?' I asked.

That's what he'd dubbed Gemma. Gemma and Brian used to go to our primary school. They'd even been friends for a whole two seconds, but Gemma was a gossip and bully, and we'd learnt to avoid her.

'I'm going to make it happen.' Brian clapped me on the shoulder with happiness.

'Make what happen?' I asked.

Gemma looked behind her guiltily. Yep, they were talking about us. I tried to eavesdrop, but their whispers were too low.

'Wait and see.'

Sabiha stopped in her tracks. 'If you care about your reputations, it's best if Jesse, Brian and I don't go to the oval,' she said in a raised voice so we could hear.

Dina grabbed her arm and gave us a fake smile. 'I don't care.'

'Yeah, I don't care,' Gemma said, less certain.

'Good.' She smiled at them.

Brian and I exchanged a look. 'I think I'll duck into the library.' I did not want to hang around where they did not want me and face snide remarks and side looks.

'Don't you dare leave me alone.' Brian yanked my arm and pushed me toward the oval. 'I need you.'

I sighed. 'Fine. But I'm not talking to them.'

'You do you. I just need you there for moral support.'

We reached the oval, and the girls determinedly walked to the other side. Why did they want to sit there? There was no shade. Sabiha sat between me and Brian, while Dina sat next to Brian and Gemma next to her. We were facing a group of boys playing soccer. What was going on?

I saw Brian watching the soccer players intently, and the penny dropped. He was going to make his debut as a soccer player today. Good. I took out my novel, *The Shining*, and began reading.

Sabiha waved at a boy on the field. I followed her gaze and saw a blond Adonis loping toward us, his torso bare and shiny with sweat. Who was he? Jealousy stung me as I saw him smiling at her.

'Hey, cuz.' He reached out and slapped Sabiha's hand in a high five.

Sabiha introduced her older cousin Adnan, who was in year eleven. Why was I so relieved that the boy was a relative? I needed to stop caring. I lifted my book back to my face and tuned out the surrounding conversation.

Sabiha nudged me in the ribs, and I looked up. Brian leapt up and took off his shirt, and folded it, leaving on his t-shirt. 'Get ready to be dazzled,' Brian said. Adnan laughed and slapped him on the back.

'Gees, he'll ruin his makeup,' Dina said. She and Gemma sniggered.

Sabiha squeezed her juice box, and her juice spilled onto Gemma, who squealed. I thought she did it accidentally until I saw the sly smile on her face.

The guys blocked Brian at first, but it didn't take them long to see his skill. Seeing his euphoria as he ran around the oval was so good. I looked back at Sabiha. It was like she was the lynchpin that had started all this. With her as a friend, we were all challenging ourselves. She watched Brian with an admiring gaze as he ran, and I quickly returned to my book, finding it hard to take.

Adnan and Brian ran over to us. 'You really can play,' Adnan said as he picked up his backpack.

'Thanks.' Brian put his shirt on.

'Same time tomorrow?' Adnan put his hand out for a high five.

'You're on.' Brian slapped his hand.

'See ya cuz,' Adnan called as he ran off.

We walked to Maths class together. We stopped and Brian got a paper towel and wiped off the mud and grass from his black leather shoes.

'You're going to have to wear more appropriate footwear.'

Brian sighed. 'Yep, it will make being stylish more difficult, but I'm up for the challenge.' He sighed happily as he looked in the mirror and combed his hair.

'You did it.' I met his gaze in the mirror.

His hair was mussed, rivulets of sweat running down his cheeks. He wiped his face, the beige foundation staining the white paper towel. He examined his face. The pimples were more prominent. 'Oh, well. I guess it's time for au naturel me to make his debut.'

He propped his bent arm on my shoulder, and his confidence buoyed me as we stood by side by side. 'Maybe high school won't be so shitty anymore, now that we're working our way up the food chain.'

I wanted to believe him. As if I'd conjured him, Joshua King walked behind us and to the urinal. Usually, he'd intimidate and stare me down, even sledge me by shoving himself into my physical space. Today, he pretended like I was invisible. Brian met my gaze in the mirror again and arched his eyebrow with a smile. Maybe Brian was right. Maybe things were on the way up.

***

I went to my locker, turned on my phone, and checked my messages. There was a message from Sarah. 'Mum took a turn. All good. Come straight after school.'

I went to the front of the school, where Sabiha was waiting. The three of us were going to Sunshine Library because it was three times bigger than the St Albans library.

'Where's Brian?' Sabiha peered around me.

'He's coming. I can't make it tonight.'

'Oh, that's too bad.' Happiness crept into her voice.

It was like she'd punched me in the gut. Shit, I was the third wheel interrupting their romance.

'I mean, we'll miss you,' Sabiha jumped in, interjecting sincerity in her voice.

'Don't worry, Sabiha, I know what you mean.' I picked up my backpack and turned to leave.

We both saw Brian approaching. 'You okay?' he asked.

'Mum's not feeling well,' I said, handing Brian a list with Stephen King and Dean R. Koontz's titles scrawled on it. 'Can you get me some books?'

I turned and walked away. That was it. I would not hang around them again. Sabiha had expressed her preference, and I would not play dumb anymore.

I hurried home, my legs aching by the time I entered the front door. Sarah met me in the hallway, still in her blue scrubs, a streak of blood on her top.

'Mum is fine.' Sarah raised her hand before I spoke. 'She accidentally took a double dose of her medication, her body temperature dropped too low, and she became unresponsive. She's been to the doctor, and she's better now.'

Mrs O'Malley came by to check on Mum every day. She'd been the one who found her unresponsive and cold to touch. She'd called Sarah and then an ambulance. Thankfully, the paramedics had given her medication to counteract the double dose, and Mum had stabilised. But it could have been a lot worse.

I went to Mum's bedroom. She was sleeping in bed; her face was more swollen than usual. I left without disturbing her and went to the kitchen. I took the pillbox off the fridge. The Wednesday dose was empty. It was Tuesday. I sighed, bowing my head. Mum must have confused the days yet again. Mental deterioration was another sign of her illness.

'I've spoken to the council. We're eligible for home help a few hours a day.' Sarah sat at the kitchen table and gestured for me to join her.

'You know Mum doesn't want that.' I got a glass of water, buying time to keep my back to her. I didn't want her to see my glassy eyes as I fought back tears.

'I know. But we can't go on like this. You need to go to school, and I need to work. We can't be with her during the day.' Sarah was trying to sound strong, but I could hear the ragged edges as she spoke through her tight throat.

My hand tightened on the glass, and it broke in my hand, shards of glass cutting in. I squeezed tighter, wanting to feel the pain.

'Jesse,' Sarah gasped, jumping out of the chair and rushing to me. She took my hand and put it under the tap, washing off the glass, then pushed me into a chair. She got the first aid kit and picked out the glass.

'What are we going to do?' I pressed my face into her side, hiding into her as I cried soundlessly.

'We'll be okay.' Sarah put her hand on my head, her voice wobbling. She finished tending to my cuts and wrapped a bandage around it. 'We'll keep going, day by day. But we need more help.' She packed up the first aid kit and threw away the used gauze.

'She won't like it.' I wiped my face.

'I don't like it either. But then there are lots of things I don't like. That's life. We just have to get on with it.'

She sounded so bitter. Usually, she kept the dark veneer hidden and maintained positivity. We both felt older than our years. Sarah didn't get to do much of what any other peers her age did. We had to take turns staying home with Mum. And even when Sarah went out with her friends, it was hit and miss. She found them immature because of their insistence on drinking to excess and wasting money. Sarah didn't have that luxury. She had to watch her cents and ensure we could pay the bills.

I noticed the dark circles under her eyes. She looked suddenly older, more fatigued, and her shoulders bowed under the weight of her responsibility. I was ashamed of myself. She'd had to deal with Mum's medical emergency by herself. She let me have my regular day and only told me when school was finished. And now she had to take care of me, too. I was being such a prick.

'I'm sorry. You shouldn't have dealt with all this yourself. You should have called me to come home.'

'No. There was no point. You couldn't do anything, and you need to maintain your normal life.' She kissed me on the top of my head and brushed my curls from my forehead, a gesture she'd mimicked from our mother. It made me feel instantly comforted.

'So do you,' I said, realising I was letting Sarah sacrifice herself for my benefit again. 'You need to enjoy yourself and not have to just do everything on your own.'

She shrugged and said nothing.

When she was seventeen years old, she'd had to be a surrogate mother to me and carer to Mum. I'd had many more opportunities than her. 'I'll get a job. That will help more.'

'We don't need more money. My wage covers it. We need more help to care for Mum. And we need to go to school and to work without worrying about her.'

I felt like the walls were closing in on me. It was like I'd had a glimmer of normal life, and then I was reminded how tied down I was. Every once in a while, I felt a ripple of anger and resentment about my situation, but I pushed it away. It wasn't Mum's fault that she got cancer. That she then developed hypothyroidism that wasn't treated until it took a wrecking ball to her life. This was my life. Mum and Sarah were my only family, and I had to treasure them.

I sat by Mum's bed, needing to watch her sleep to reassure myself she was still alive. Sarah went to have a shower and lay down in bed. She looked depleted now that the adrenaline had worn off. I had homework I could do, but I was too tired, feeling brain fog. Instead, I stared out the window over Mum's body, my eyes drooping as I lightly dozed in the chair. I woke half an hour later and eased out of Mum's room and into the kitchen. We had cauliflower that I quickly sauteed and put to boil for a cauliflower soup, checking on Mum periodically.

'Go lie down,' Sarah said from the doorway.

I glanced at the clock. Two hours had passed since I came home. I stretched my arms up and moved my neck. 'I'm okay.' I kept my voice low so as not to disturb Mum. 'I dozed a little.'

'I'll make dinner.'

'I've got it under control.'

Sarah smiled and shook her head. Mum stirred in the bed, and we both approached. Her eyes opened slowly, clouded with confusion.

'Hey, Mum. You had a bit of a turn,' Sarah said gently, taking her hand. 'But you're going to be alright.'

'I don't remember.' Mum looked between us, her eyes wide with panic as she tried to capture those forgotten memories.

'That's perfectly natural. Just a side effect from the medication,' Sarah continued, smiling reassuringly.

Mum took her at her word and nodded.

'How are you feeling?' I pushed my chair closer.

'Tired.' Mum blinked sleepily.

'Let's have some dinner, and you can go back to sleep.' Sarah helped Mum sit up, lodging pillows behind her while I went to serve the soup. I brought a tray table we set up across Mum's lap and then two more trays for Sarah and me to eat in Mum's room. Sarah switched on the television to Home and Away, and we sipped our soup as we watched, the bright light of the TV casting a glow in the room as the sun set.

Mum took a few spoons and then became listless, her hand wobbling. I took her spoon and spooned it into her mouth. She looked at me helplessly. I could see her apology in her eyes.

'It's okay, Mum. That's what family is for. To take care of each other.' A tear slid down her eye and I wiped it away, kissing her on the cheek.

We finished the episode, and I took the dishes out, washing them in the kitchen, while Sarah got a bucket of warm water and a washcloth, closing Mum's bedroom as she gave her a hospital bath. Sarah finished, and we both trudged to our bedrooms, the day's emotion weighing us down. I wanted to help Sarah check on Mum throughout the night and left my bedroom door open, even though she had an internal alarm clock after doing night-shifts and would wake up every two hours, regardless. As I went to bed, feeling like I'd had a ton of bricks land on top of me. I woke up in a panic at two am. My bedroom door was closed. Sarah, wanting to leave me sleeping. I pushed my bedding out of the way and opened the door, stalking over to Mum's room. Light spilled from the hallway onto her bed, her chest rising evenly. I breathed out a sigh of relief. I heard the patter of footsteps behind me. My panicked movements had disturbed Sarah.

'Nightmare?' she asked.

I nodded. They'd started soon after Mum was diagnosed with cancer. Over the years they'd recede, but whenever something happened, they re-started. It was always the same dream. Sarah and I stood over Mum's casket as it was lowered into a grave. In the dream, I was always ten years old, the age I was when Mum was first diagnosed, and I was screaming for her to return, while Sarah held me back from falling into the grave.

Sarah walked over and hugged me from behind. 'She's okay.'

I nodded. 'Go sleep. I'll stay up with her.'

Sarah sighed heavily. She knew better than to change my mind. I could not sleep, anyway. I sat in the armchair beside Mum's bed, covering myself with a blanket, and dozed. Sarah came to check on Mum at four am and urged me to bed.

Sarah woke me at eight am. I looked at her, bleary-eyed and heavy-headed. She wore scrubs, her hair tied back in a ponytail. 'I'm going to work.'

'Are you sure?' I asked. There were still dark circles under her eyes. She had slept little.

She shrugged. She had to save her sick days as much as possible. There were always appointments or viruses she had to stay home from.

'I'm going to stay home.' My cut hand felt sore. I'd slept heavily in the early morning, trapping it under my torso, and now it felt hot and heavy. I also wanted to monitor Mum.

Sarah nodded, unsurprised. I had a little more leeway from high school. Mum and I spent a quiet day at home. I cleaned the house in the morning and made us sandwiches, noting our dwindling supplies. Mum stayed in bed, and we ate lunch together as we watched her daytime soapie. I went grocery shopping while Mrs O'Malley stayed with Mum for an hour.

In the afternoon, there was a knock on the door. I opened it and found Brian holding a canvas bag in his hand. 'Are you okay?'

I put my finger on my lips. Mum's bedroom door was right next to the front door. We tiptoed to my bedroom, and I left the door ajar. 'Mum took a double dose of her medication. She's okay now, just woozy.'

'What about you?' Brian asked.

I said nothing. He sat beside me on the bed, putting his arm around my shoulder. He'd been with me since Mum's cancer diagnosis and knew sometimes no words were needed.

'How did everything go today?' I asked after I'd collected myself.

'That reminds me.' He bent down and picked up his backpack, rifling through it, before handing me sheaves of paper. 'Here are your notes and all the homework.'

'Really? You did all this?' Brian was not known for his school organisation skills.

'Not quite.'

I looked at the notes and recognised Sabiha's handwriting. A warm glow filled me. She'd actually thought about me. I hadn't thought about our last interaction and how it made me feel, but it eased the sting. This was atonement or genuine friendship. Either way, I felt supported and appreciated.

'Thanks, Brian. I'll thank Sabiha tomorrow.'

'Here are your library books, too.' He took them from his backpack and stacked them on my desk table.

'How did everything go at the library?' Had their relationship progressed without me as a third wheel?

'All good. That girl reads more than you. She borrowed so many books she couldn't carry them.' Brian's voice was light and teasing. They were still friends, still friendly.

I don't know why I was so relieved. It was none of my business. 'Do you want to play a game?' I reached for my controller.

'Fuck yes.'

I tossed him the second controller, and we played for an hour, allowing me to zone out for a while.

'You know, I think I've realised something.'

I glanced at him sideways, his serious tone catching me off guard. He was sitting up straight, his hands tight on the controller as he stared rigidly at the screen.

'I think I like boys.' He took a deep breath. 'I mean, I definitely like boys.'

'Okay.' I shrugged. 'Any boy in particular?'

Brian nodded jerkily.

'Good. I'm happy for you.'

Brian bit his lip. 'You don't mind.'

I paused the game on the controller and turned to him. 'I don't give a shit. You're my best friend, and I love you.'

Brian paused the game too, and finally met my eyes. There was such pain in his brown eyes that my stomach clenched.

'You promise?'

'I promise.' I reached out and hugged him. He held me tight, sobs heaving his chest. I knew what it cost him to come out.

Brian lifted his face, and I reached for the tissue box on my bedside table. 'You're the only one who knows.'

I nodded. His father would not take the news well.

'I tried telling Sabiha about me.' He took a tissue and wiped his face.

I tensed. I'd been so focused on Brian and supporting him, I hadn't even thought through the implications. If Brian was gay, then Sabiha was no longer his love interest.

I bit my lip. 'What did you say?'

'That I wear makeup.' Brian looked up from his dark eyelashes.

'Yeah, but that means nothing. Lots of guys wear makeup.'

'That's what she said.' Brian said.

'So it's not really a hint then, is it?' I had to be delicate and not let my desire cloud my judgement. This was about Brian and supporting him.

'We're in the friendship zone now anyway, so it doesn't matter?' he said.

I wanted to ask him if Sabiha knew but stilled my tongue.

Brian clicked the buttons and re-started the game. We played for a few minutes, the only sound in the room was the shooting from the screen. 'What if she won't be my friend anymore?'

'I think she will. Sabiha isn't a homophobe.' I hoped I wasn't giving him the wrong advice, for both our sakes. If Sabiha didn't accept him, then I would have to choose my best friend.

Brian kept playing, not looking at me. Finally, he nodded. 'I know you're right. I'm going to tell her soon.'

'Okay.' I just had to be patient and wait. This was Brian's news to tell. 'Who's the boy?'

Brian smiled, his brown eyes sparkling. 'He is firmly in the closet, but he is so tasty.'

I laughed, happy at his joy. It's like something had loosened inside him now that he'd come out. He spent the rest of the game extolling the virtues of his crush, and I realised he'd never been able to talk about who he liked. I just hoped his secret crush liked him back.

Chapter 4

The next morning I saw Sabiha waiting out the front of school. As Brian and I crossed the street, we both waved.

Brian kissed her on the cheek. 'You're early today.'

Sabiha looked at me. I wanted more than anything to lean in and kiss her on the cheek, to breathe in her scent, and that's why I couldn't. Until Brian came out to her, I couldn't muddy the waters. I had to bide my time and be patient.

'How's your Mum?' she asked.

'Good.' I stared at my feet.

I saw her frown at Brian, who shrugged. *Stop being weird, Jesse. She's your friend. Your friend.* I wanted to thank her for taking down notes but hesitated, and the conversation had moved on.

'Why are you early?' Brian asked her as we walked to our bench.

'I can be on time.' She climbed on the bench, and we followed. Sitting on the table with our feet on the bench in our usual formation, me, Brian, and then Sabiha.

Brian took off his backpack and threw it on the stool. 'Not that I've seen.'

'I did my Maths homework. You can copy my notes.'

'Who are you?' He peered into her face. 'What did you do to the real Sabiha Omerović?' He lifted her hair and looked into her ear.

I watched, envious of their easy affection. I wished I could act like that with her.

Sabiha laughed. 'Do you want to see?'

'You betcha.' Brian tickled her waist. ''Cause I don't believe you did it.'

She unzipped her backpack and searched it. 'It's here.'

'Sure, sure.' Brian patted her head.

She jerked away. 'It is.' She tipped everything onto the table and checked each notebook. 'I left it in the library.'

'Are you sure the dog didn't eat it?' I forced myself into the conversation. I needed to stop being so awkward.

'Smartarse,' she muttered.

'Let's go and look.' Brian gestured for her to lead the way.

'Miss Swan!' Sabiha called out as she ran to the counter.

'Looking for this?' Miss Swan held out a notebook.

Sabiha smiled and hugged it to her chest. 'Thanks heaps.' She turned to give Brian and me a triumphant look.

'It was a pleasure having your company this morning, Sabiha,' Miss Swan said.

'I wonder why a girl who can't be on time to class would be early to school? Are you blushing?' He peered at her cheek as we walked out of the library. 'Perhaps she has a new crush she's stalking?' Brian nudged me suggestively.

I jerked back in surprise. Did Sabiha have a crush on someone?

'No, I wanted to avoid the crowds,' Sabiha said sarcastically.

Brian and I guffawed. My laugh was mostly triggered by relief and hope that she and Brian had definitely moved into the friendship zone.

Brian cupped his ear. 'We have a late-breaking announcement. Sabiha Omerović, a sixteen-year-old schoolgirl from St Albans, Victoria, woke at the crack of dawn and scurried to school to avoid the monstrous crowds at peak hour.'

I smiled as I watched him inhabit the character of a newscaster.

'Congestion peaked at 8.30 a.m., but thankfully no one was crushed to death. Keep tuned, and we'll have more updates later.' Brian shifted his eyes from side to side as if he was reading a teleprompter. 'And now we go to Jesse James, our on-location correspondent, who has a live interview with our fearful schoolgirl.' Brian turned to me.

'When did you develop this fear of crowds?' I thrust an imaginary microphone in Sabiha's face.

'Piss off!' She pushed my hand away and ran to class.

'I didn't mean to—' I said to Brian, horrified that I'd blundered and made her angry.

'It's not your fault, bro. It must be her time of the month.' He put his arm around my shoulders, and we walked to class together.

I nodded, my mind turning back to our earlier conversation. 'You said earlier she had a crush?'

'Sabiha has many crushes. She's a bigger perv than me.' Brian waved his hand.

I was surprised. I thought she and Brian were heading into the more than friends' territory before he realised he was gay. 'But I thought the two of you liked each other?'

'Of course we like each other. She's my best friend. I mean, we're all best friends,' he quickly interjected, not wanting me to think she'd overtaken my position.

'But you're all touchy-feely with each other?' Their PDA was constant, and from the sidelines, it looked like they were more than friends.

'I think we've entered the friend zone.'

I nodded, trying to process. I thought that the only obstacle in my path was Brian's claim on Sabiha. But now she might have other crushes. Where did this leave me?

'Why are you asking?' Brian scrutinised me. 'Wait, do you like her?'

I hurried away, my cheeks flushing.

Brian caught up to me. 'Because you have the all clear. Anyway, the two of you would be kind of perfect together. You both have so much in common.'

I glanced at him. That's exactly what I'd been thinking. Maybe there was hope if he thought so, too.

'Don't worry, I've got your back.' Brian slapped my shoulder. 'I'll clear the way for you.'

At recess, Brian and I returned to the front of the school to hang out with Sabiha, but she didn't show. My shoulders slumped as self-consciousness descended. 'This is my fault.'

'No, it's not. You did nothing wrong.' Brian was crushing a tree leaf and throwing it to the ground. 'She seriously needs to develop a thicker skin.'

I spent the rest of the morning down in the dumps. In fourth period we were together again for history. Instead of sitting in her usual spot in the back row with Brian and me, she sat in the middle row.

Brian watched her with furious eyes. She squirmed in her seat as if she could feel his anger scorching her back. He tore out a page of his notebook and scrawled something on it, tapping the person in front of him to pass it to Sabiha. Gordana was behind Sabiha and passed a note.

Sabiha read it and turned and stared at Brian. He stared back.

She wrote a reply and sent it back. Over the next ten minutes, they kept scrawling messages back and forth. At one point, Sabiha looked at me. I tried to shake myself out of the dumps and sat up straighter, trying to wipe the mopey look off my face. She didn't need to know how much she'd cut me.

We met at the door when class finished and walked together to our usual bench. Lunch was subdued. I avoided speaking to her. I would not fall for the trap again of relaxing my guard, only to have her stomp on me.

'You two have English together now, don't you?' Brian said when the bell rang. 'I'm off to Science.' He headed down the corridor.

I stood next to Sabiha like a lump of wood. Shit, I hadn't thought this through. Now I had to go to class with her, and there would be no Brian to be a buffer. I was full of dread. This was going to be so awkward.

'Let's get going,' Sabiha said cheerfully.

We sat in our usual seat next to the window. I concentrated on the teacher's instructions. When we had to pair and share, I looked slightly over Sabiha's shoulder, not wanting to make eye contact. She got the hint and kept it all professional.

The classroom warmed, and Sabiha took off her jumper. As I went to write in my notebook, her arm was next to me. There were dark bruises in the shape of a handprint. Someone must have held her viciously and tightly to cause such a bruise.

'What happened?' I asked.

'I fell.' She put her jumper back on, looking around the class to see if anyone else had noticed.

'Is that the reason you came to school early?' I pushed.

She didn't respond, pretending she was engrossed in copying the teacher's notes. I surreptitiously watched her during the lesson. As the clock ticked down to the end of class and going home time, Sabiha tensed further and further. Her hands clenched her pencil so tightly she snapped it in two. She was scared. Something must have happened after school.

Rage suffused me. Did Joshua King go after her? I was going to kill the fucker.

When the bell rang, she shot up and ran for the door. I ran after her, but she weaved through the crowd too quickly. I ran to the third floor and the Science rooms. Brian was strolling down the corridor.

'Come on, we have to catch up to Sabiha. I know why she was early this morning.' Brian kept pace with me. 'I think she was bashed. She had bruises all up and down her arms.'

'I'm going to kill King.' Brian leapt down the steps, taking three at a time, and I now had to catch up to him.

We caught up to King at the lockers. I shoved him hard into the metal lockers. 'Did you touch Sabiha?' I demanded.

'Woah, I did nothing to her.' King looked shocked, his hands lifted in surrender.

Anton shoved himself between us. 'He didn't touch your girl! Promise!'

I looked back at Brian. He looked as confused as I felt. I thought for sure that King was responsible. If he didn't hurt Sabiha, then who did?

'Good.' Brian leaned into Joshua's face. 'Make sure you stay away from her.'

We waited for Joshua and Anton to leave. 'Who did it then?' I asked.

Brian shook his head dumbly. 'I guess we're going to have to ask her.'

We waited for her at the school gates. 'Let me see,' Brian demanded as soon as she was in earshot.

'What?' Sabiha played dumb.

Brian grabbed her top and lifted it.

I couldn't believe he was being so forward. Sabiha didn't seem thrown by it. She slapped his hand away and wrenched her top down. 'Arsehole.' She looked nervously at the students walking past.

'Let me see,' Brian insisted.

'Fine.' She stomped behind the bushes, and we followed. She lifted her top.

Brian whistled between his teeth as he gently touched her skin. 'Those are beauties.'

My stomach dropped. She had large bruises on her torso. Someone had really done a number on her. She looked so small and vulnerable. I was torn between wanting to take her in my arms to comfort her and pummelling someone until I assuaged my killing rage.

'Who was it?' I demanded.

She pulled her top down and stood between us, looking lost.

A terrible thought popped into my head.

'Was it your Mum?' I asked softly into the silence.

'As if,' she laughed.

I was relieved. That would be the worst thing. To have to go home to that environment every night.

'Who was it?' I persisted.

'Some girls.' She waved her hand dismissively.

Even though I'd thought Joshua was telling the truth, I was relieved to have it confirmed.

'That's why you came to school early?' Brian asked.

She nodded, on the verge of tears. Brian put his arm around her. 'I'm such a loser,' she said into his shoulder.

I cursed myself. I'd wanted to take her into my arms, but we were still so stiff and formal with each other. Brian was so effortlessly tactile. It made me jealous.

'My bully was Tommy Jones in Fifth Grade,' Brian said.

'Mine was Joe O'Shea in Year Seven,' I said, skipping Joshua King. He didn't count since I'd vanquished him.

She laughed. 'We're all losers.' She found a tissue in her pocket.

'Stay away from them,' Brian said.

'No shit Shirl.' I screwed up the tissue in my hand.

'Who are they?' I asked.

'Bitches who live in the next street from my house.' She blew her nose.

'You're stuffed,' Brian said.

I shot him a dirty look. He shrugged, giving off the 'what can we do' vibe.

'I know.' Sabiha chucked the tissue at a bin and missed.

'We'll walk you home tonight.' I needed to make sure she was safe. I didn't want anyone to hurt her again.

'Really?' she asked Brian.

Brian nodded. 'We'll catch the bus back.'

She hugged him. 'Thank you,' she whispered into Brian's ear. She opened her eyes and gave me a gummy smile. 'You're the best.'

I smiled back. We would have to work up to hugs.

'Which way do we go?' Brian asked.

'Straight down Main Road West.' She pointed.

The train tracks divided Main Road into East and West. Brian and I lived on the east side of St Albans, while Sabiha lived on the other side. We chatted about school as we walked, but as we crossed over the train tracks, Sabiha clammed up, jamming her hands in her pants as she looked around warily, like she was expecting the boogeyman to jump out at her.

I sidled closer to her, our hands brushing against each other. All I had to do was reach and take her hand in mine. This was the perfect time to break the ice.

Brian put his arm around her waist and pulled her toward him. 'We're here with you.'

I jammed my hand back in my pocket, taking a deep breath. I had to be quicker and stop second-guessing myself.

Sabiha looked at us wildly, panic on her face. She stopped on the footpath. 'You can turn back now.'

Brian put his hand on her shoulder. 'We don't mind.'

She clasped Brian's hand. 'You've gone so far out of your way.'

'What if they're waiting for you near your house?' We'd come so far. I had to make sure she was home safe.

'I don't want you caught up in this bullshit.' She fisted her hands by her side.

I searched her face. She thought we were wusses. That we weren't up to defending her from two girls. My cheeks became hot. 'I'm not scared of stupid girls.'

'I know you're not.' Her voice was flat, revealing her doubt.

Brian smiled. 'We've been bullied by worse.' He turned her to face Main Road West.

Brian took her hand in his and walked with her while I hung back. How was he not pissed off by this? She was insulting our manhood.

When we got to her corner, she waved across the street. 'There's the bus stop.'

Brian nodded and surveyed her street. 'We'll walk you to your house.'

When we were two houses away, she stopped. 'You can go back now because I don't want my mum to know.'

Brian kissed her on the cheek. 'I'll see you at school.'

'Thanks guys,' she said.

I turned and walked off.

'Wait up,' Brian shouted.

When we'd reached a large elm tree a few houses away, I stopped and turned, watching Sabiha walk the last few steps to her house and up the driveway. I needed to know she was safe.

'You know she meant nothing by it,' Brian said.

'She didn't mean to call us wusses who couldn't stand up to two girls. Doesn't that piss you off?' I gestured back down the street.

'Nah. I know what we did. We made Joshua King back down. We can take on anyone.' Brian bounced around, lifting his fists as if he was punching an imaginary opponent. 'Anyway, Sabiha isn't known for her tact. It's what I love about her. She's a dead-set bitch.'

I burst out laughing. 'Seriously?'

'Yep. She's just the right combination of brutal honesty and a complete lack of boundaries. You never have to wonder what she's thinking or feeling. She'll tell you to your face.'

I mulled that over as we walked toward the bus stop. Maybe I needed to stop inferring Sabiha's motives and accept her at face value. She thought of me as a friend. That's what we were. Now it was up to me to get her to see me as something more.

I smiled as we sat on the bus and travelled home. This was eminently doable. I had to do something big. Something that would make her see me differently. I leaned my head on the seat as I thought.

I reached my house and checked the mailbox, finding a large A4 envelope. As I took it out, feeling the heavy cardboard under my fingers, my stomach fluttered with anticipation. Could this be? I peeled open the envelope and took out the magazine. Yes. I quickly tucked it into my backpack. This was news I wanted to savour and share with Sarah and Mum.

When I arrived home, Mum was in the living room watching her TV shows. She smiled and greeted me. Marian, a matronly woman with curly grey hair, appeared in the hallway, wiping her hands on the tea towel. After Mum's mishap with the medication last week, Sarah had arranged for a council worker to come in and be with Mum every day while we were at school. Marian was allocated, and she and Mum had become steadfast companions.

I followed Marian into the kitchen. 'How was she today?'

'She had a good day.' Marian opened the oven door and took out a tray. On it was a crumbed fish fillet and potatoes. 'We watched her stories at lunchtime together, and while she was napping, I popped in here and got this ready.'

My mouth salivated. It had been years since I had come home to a cooked meal. I looked at the kitchen sink in wonder. There were no dishes to do. Marian had washed them and put them away. Through the kitchen window, I saw the full clothesline.

My eyes teared up.' You didn't have to do all this.'

Marian approached and hugged me. 'This is my job. I'm here to take care of you.'

I bent down and hugged her back, her soft body reminding me of hugging Mum.

Marian broke the hug. 'There's cut-up snacks in the fridge and a salad for dinner.'

I nodded, not trusting myself to speak. Marian said goodbye to Mum, and the front door closed behind her.

I got the plate of veggies she'd cut up and sat in the living room with Mum. She was in high spirits, regaling me with the highlights of her soapie and what she and Marian talked about. Sarah had been right after all. We needed help. Marian was at home with Mum all day. She completed the domestic chores and was Mum's companion, which meant I could come home and just focus on my schoolwork. The weight on my shoulders was slowly lifting, making me realise how heavy the burden of being a carer had been.

After we finished the snacks, I took the plate to the kitchen and washed it, before going to the carport. I rifled at the back and found Sarah's bike. She used to ride it to school and her part-time job at Hungry Jack's until she turned eighteen and could drive Mum's car. It had been collecting dust and rust in the carport in the four years since. I wheeled it to the middle of the carport and turned it upside down, cleaning it and checking the brakes.

Sarah pulled into the driveway and walked over. 'All good?' She glanced at the house.

'Mum had a good day. Spending the day with Marian is really doing her good.'

Sarah smiled in relief.

'And she made dinner.'

'Wow.' Sarah was finding our new routine as wonder-inducing as I was.

'Do you mind if I give your bike to Sabiha? She's having some trouble with transport to and from home.' I knew Sabiha didn't want anyone knowing about her being bashed, and even though Sarah was my sister, it felt like breaking a confidence.

'Of course. It's not doing me any good.'

I wiped my hands on a rag, and we walked into the house together.

'So you and Sabiha are progressing to the gifts stage of your friendship?' Sarah lifted an eyebrow as I followed her to the living room.

I glared at her.

'What are you hoping she'll gift you in return?'

I reached to punch her in the arm, but she ran into the living room, where Mum lifted her head from the couch.

'Jesse, stop tormenting your sister,' Mum said sternly.

Sarah and I stuttered to a stop, gaping at each other in wonder. This was the first time Mum had sounded like herself in years. We'd been her carers for so long that it seemed as if she'd deferred all parental authority.

'Of course,' I murmured, a big grin on my face. Marian was a positive influence on us all.

Chapter 5

The next morning, Brian knocked at the front door. I went to the carport and got the bike.

'You will not ride that!' he exclaimed, examining the purple V-shape that signified it was a girl's bike.

'It's for Sabiha so she can get home safely.' I'd woken up early and used the light to finish getting it ready.

'That's a great idea. Where did you get it?'

'It's Sarah's. It's been rusting for years.'

Brian looked at me knowingly.

'What?' I demanded defensively, my cheeks heating. 'It's what I would do for any of my friends.'

'I said nothing.' He smiled knowingly.

I kicked a rock near my foot, my cheeks becoming even hotter. Damn my complexion.

We headed to school, and I pushed the bike beside me.

'Gimme a ride.' Brian took the handlebars and took a few spins on the road before coming back next to me. 'Your turn.'

I took the bike and took a few spins before riding along next to Brian.

'My turn.' He jumped on. We turned the corner and were onto Main Road. He soon zipped in and out of the crowd.

I waited for him to return and saw him up ahead, riding through the front gates. Bastard. I picked up my pace. When I arrived, Brian was handing the bike to Sabiha.

As I approached, he pulled me into a bear hug. 'Where were you?'

I punched him on the arm, a little harder than usual. 'We were supposed to swap riding the bike to school.' I'd wanted to be the conquering hero and hand Sabiha the bike that would save her. See her smile at me and think of me differently. Instead, Brian stole my limelight.

Brian gave me a cheeky smile. 'I like the fast life.'

I turned to Sabiha. 'Do you like it?' I asked with a shy smile.

'I love it.' She stopped short. Her face contorted as if she was figuring out an impossible Maths equation. 'I—, I don't—.' She glanced at Brian, pleading.

Brian took pity on her. 'She doesn't know if she can take it for free.'

'And I have no money to pay for it,' she added.

I deflated. So much for the conquering hero. I'd hoped she'd be impressed, instead she was worried about being beholden to me. Shit, how was I going to smooth this over?

'How about a trade?'

'Okay.' She looked at me suspiciously.

Come up with something. Come up with something, James.
'Bring in your CDs so I can load them onto my computer.' I breathed out a sigh of relief.

'That can't be the trade for a bike,' she said.

I nearly groaned in frustration. I'd never had to work so hard to give someone a gift. 'That's your fee for borrowing it for a year.'

'Really?'

I shrugged. 'It was rusting in the backyard since my sister bought a car.' I downplayed the work I'd had to do to get it ready.

'Thanks.' She kissed me on the cheek.

I blushed. I'd been hoping for a token of affection, for us to relax with each other, yet now that she'd kissed me, I was embarrassed. 'It was nothing.' I put my hand through my hair.

'I'd better get going.' I needed a time-out. I could still feel the imprint of her lips on my cheek and wanted nothing more than to grab her and kiss her back.

'Where are you off to?' Brian asked.

'Gotta do something,' I mumbled and stalked off to the three-storey building. As soon as I entered, I leaned my back against the wall, panting. What a disaster. When I'd played out the scene in my mind last night, I'd imagined walking up to her and giving her the bike, making a declaration about how I wanted to make sure she was safe. I would impress her, her eyes watering with tears and gratitude, and then she'd hug me. Somehow the hug would become a kiss, and then... My thoughts trailed off. I glanced around to see if anyone was watching.

Instead, my entire plan was ruined, firstly by Brian jumping the gun and handing her the bike and then by Sabiha's reluctance to accept it. I don't know why I'd cast Sabiha in the role of a grateful and meek maiden. She was anything but. I'd thought this would be the gesture that would turn the tide. And it had.

I touched my cheek where she'd kissed it. She'd kissed me! It was the first time we touched. I needed to look at the positives. My plan had worked. Now I just needed to make a grander gesture. Something more spectacular that she couldn't misinterpret.

I drifted to the library. Charlie was in his usual spot in the corner, wearing headphones and dark sunglasses to deal with sensory overload. He found the public school system overwhelming, but he kept persisting. His parents didn't want to put him in a special school. He had too much potential, they said.

Charlie nodded at me but didn't pause as his hand deftly moved over his sketchpad. What could I do to get Sabiha to see me? Really see me. I watched Charlie sketching, his face looking like he was transported to another world. I needed something that reflected me. Something that was a gift: a story, a book, a love story. The idea hit me like an earthquake.

I waved my hand under Charlie's eyes. I knew not to touch him to get his attention. He startled when anyone touched him.

'Do you want to write a book together?'

Charlie nodded.

'But it's going to be a love story.'

'A zombie love story.' Charlie loved drawing, but he only drew one thing: zombies.

'Yes, a zombie love story. About a boy who loves a girl, and he has to save her from all these dangers, but she doesn't see him as a hero. She's pretty bad arse and can save herself. But she learns that the two of them are better together. And he keeps trying to get her to see him for more than a zombie. But she doesn't. And then, finally, one day she sees that he's the one. And they fall in love.'

'But she's a human, and he's a zombie. How's that going to work? He'll eat her.' Charlie was literal. In his world, zombies ate humans and there was no changing that one defining rule.

I thought for a minute, letting the story settle in my mind, remembering what Brian had said that Sabiha and I had so much in common. But still, she was so much cooler than me and didn't see us on the same level. 'Yes, but she's a zombie too. She just didn't accept her true self. It's only when she falls in love with him she can truly accept herself and they can be together.'

Charlie nods. 'That works.'

'And I know who I want the girl to look like.' I led him to the library window. The bench we hung out at the front of the school was visible. Brian and Sabiha were sitting on the table facing us, the two of them laughing and animated.

'I want the girl to look like her.' I pointed to Sabiha.

Charlie nodded. 'And he's the boy.'

'No, I'm the boy. I'm the boy who loves her and wants her to love me back.'

Charlie nodded, saying nothing. That's what I loved about him. He wasn't prone to filling the silence with small talk or platitudes. He accepted everyone as they were.

This plan was going to work. Sabiha would read the graphic novel, and she'd get it. She'd know that I was the one for her, and she was the one for me.

Our lunchtime ritual had developed into eating lunch on the oval while Adnan and Brian played soccer. Today they skipped their game, and we all sat on the grass next to the soccer pitch, Dina and Gemma joining us. There was a weird energy at the school as parent—teacher night approached.

'Have you booked your meetings?' Brian asked.

'I only get them to meet my favourite teachers and ignore the rest,' Dina said.

'What about when they get reports?' I asked.

'Nah, they expect me to do well but don't know enough about the school system to take an interest. It's the only perk of having Non-English-speaking parents. They'll meet the teachers who confirm what they want to hear, and we're all happy.' She smiled ruefully.

'My Mum gets a copy of my timetable at the beginning of the semester and checks off that she's met with everyone,' Brian said. 'I think I'm failing Geography.'

I was worried about him. I knew what his dad was like. He was just waiting for an excuse to push him into a tradie apprenticeship. Brian's poor grades might give him that. Even though Brian acted relaxed, I knew he was stressed and on edge.

'I think I'm failing Maths, History and Phys Ed,' Gemma interrupted.

'How do you fail Phys Ed?' Sabiha asked.

'I dunno,' Gemma said.

Sabiha rolled her eyes. I caught her gaze.

'What about you?' she asked me.

'My sister's coming tonight,' I said.

'What about your mum and dad?' Gemma asked.

'My Dad's dead, and Mum isn't feeling well.' I'd delivered this story so often that the excuse rolled off my tongue. It was all technically true. 'What about you?' I asked Sabiha.

'Mum doesn't really care about my achievements at school. She's got health issues.'

'What health issues?' My ears pricked. Did we have something else in common?

Sabiha opened her mouth to answer, but the conversation moved on when Adnan shook his head dismissively, and Gemma caught him and said, 'You have nothing to worry about, Einstein.'

Adnan had featured in the school newspaper as the high achiever in his year level.

'Capitalism breeds pride in mediocrity,' Adnan spat out.

I hid a smile. Trust the communist in the group to find a way to put down everyone here, as well as the whole economic system of Western society. I could tell by the blank faces around me that no one else understood his esoteric putdown. I muffled a chuckle behind my hand.

Everyone else looked at Sabiha. She was his cousin, and they expected her to stand up to him. 'What's up your arse?' she burst out.

He eyeballed the group with scorn. 'You have every opportunity to be what you want, to achieve anything you want, and all you do is brag about how to avoid hard work.' He stood. 'In Yugoslavia, anyone would be ashamed to fail a class, let alone repeat a year; yet here, it's cool.'

'Who the fuck died and made you king?' Sabiha asked. 'Arsehole,' she called as he pivoted on his heel and left.

'It's not his fault,' Dina said.

'Just because you like him doesn't mean you have to make excuses for him,' Sabiha said.

'It can't be easy. His Mum and sister are the breadwinners in the family since his dad can't work,' Dina insisted heatedly.

'His whole family depends on him to achieve something with his life.'

'He's still an arsehole.'

It surprised me to hear Dina's defence. I'd thought of Adnan as the golden boy, the Adonis of the group. He effortlessly flitted around the school, being both the jock with his soccer prowess and the intellectual by achieving top grades. Hangers-on always surrounded him and he had a flashing smile on his face like he was walking to his jet. I didn't realise how hard his life was. I looked at Sabiha and wondered what else he didn't know about her. What health issues did her mother suffer from? I needed to make more of an effort to get to know her.

Brian invited Adnan, Sabiha, and me to his house after school until the interviews began. I walked with Sabiha to get her bike while Adnan and Brian waited at the front. 'Give me the key.'

She handed me the key, and I unlocked the padlock, which was locked near the bike chain; the grease covering my hands.

'Sorry.'

'It's OK.' I pulled out tissues and wiped my hands.

'You've got to be the only guy in the world who carries tissues.'

'It's to give to the girls that I make cry.' I relaxed in her company for the first time. Knowing she too might face the same burdens as me made me feel at ease. Maybe her tough exterior was a coping mechanism?

She laughed and felt my stomach warm. I made her laugh.

Brian and Adnan walked ahead, leaving us to follow. 'Here.' I took the bike from her and wheeled it beside me with one hand.

'I can do that.'

'But I can do it better. I'm reading a brilliant book at the moment.' I reached into my backpack with the other hand. The front cover was black with a line of red hearts to the title that read, *The Messenger*. 'It's an amazing book. Everyone's raving about it. I've read other books by Markus Zusak, but this is the best.'

I watched her as she read the blurb, her green eyes intense, a small frown between her eyebrows as she concentrated.

'It sounds great.' She went to hand it back. 'I'll have to chase it up at the library.'

'Keep it,' I said. 'I've already read it.' This way, we'd have something to talk about. This could be a scene in the zombie love story. The boy could give the zombie girl weapons because she wants to fight.

'Thanks.' She put it in her backpack.

I was trying to think of a way to segue into her mother's health issues, when some boys from our Phys Ed class walked past. 'Hey Jesse, you want to play dodgeball?' They all laughed.

I blushed. Pricks. While Joshua King and Anton steered clear and left me alone during Phys Ed, some of them were still assholes. Most of the time it didn't bother me, but now with Sabiha, it was awkward.

She was avoiding looking at me. 'Why don't you tell them off?' she burst out.

'Why?' I said. 'So they can have a go at me again? Anyway, they'll get their own.'

'When you kill them?'

'I've already killed them,' I said with a sly smile. I was trying to look funny but regretted it as her face blanched.

'Here, look—' I quickly reached into my backpack and handed her a magazine, *Voiceworks*.

'I don't get it.'

I took it back from her and turned to the title page. She read the item above my index finger. '*Massacre* by Jesse James.' She flipped to page twenty-two and read the first line. 'You wrote a short story?'

I nodded shyly. 'Yeah, and I found this magazine that only publishes writers under twenty-five.'

I'd been so happy when I came home yesterday to find my copy of the magazine in the mail. I was a published writer. It was such a buzz. I'd only shown it to Sarah and Mum, who

made a big deal and made me read it out loud during dinner.
They clapped afterwards. When Brian came over, I showed it to
him. He'd congratulated me in a low-key way. But now, Sabiha
was reading it. I was a nervous wreck. I hopped on the bike
and wheeled round and round, trying to work off my nervous
energy.

'Wow, it's amazing.' She was looking at me differently. Finally,
I could see things changing.

'Thanks.' I returned the magazine back in his bag, suddenly
shy under her admiration.

'Why didn't you tell anyone?'

I shrugged, looking away.

'If people knew about this, they'd leave you alone. You're so
talented.'

I smiled.

'Have you had other things published?'

I nodded. She kept interrogating me as I told her about my
other success in the local council short story competition. She
was even more amazed.

'I write a bit too. I've only submitted them to Miss Partridge,
though!' She laughed quickly. 'But I've sometimes thought
about doing more.'

'You can. My sister got me a membership from Writers'
Victoria. They send out a newsletter every month with a listing
of short story competitions and places to submit. You can read
my back issues.'

This was my in. This was the way I could get close to her. Get
the zombie girl to realise she was a zombie too. 'If you want.'
I cleared my throat. 'I can read your stories and tell you what I
think.'

'Really?'

'And maybe you can read my stories before I submit them,
too. We can be critique partners.' I continued, as my plan
snapped into place.

'You want *my* feedback? But you're a much better writer. You've been published and everything.'

'My sister used to proofread for me, but now she's busy with uni.' I lied. Sarah still always read my stories, but I needed to stretch the truth and make sure she wanted to spend time with me.

'I'd love to!'

'Jesse!' Sarah called from in front of the house across the street.

I handed Sabiha the bike. 'I'll bring that stuff we talked about to school.' I hesitated, wanting to say something more.

Sarah saw the bike and realised who I was with.

'You must be Sabiha,' she said as she approached and introduced herself. She rested her arm on my shoulder. 'He's told us about you.'

My cheeks reddened. Damn it, Sarah. She was going to ruin it all. 'Let's go, Sarah.' I steered her toward the house before she could say anything else. 'We have to leave soon.'

'Would you like to come in?' Sarah asked Sabiha.

Brian called out to her. He and Adnan were waiting for her at the end of the street.

'She has to go,' I said, relieved we had a reprieve.

'Another time.' Sarah made it sound like a date.

'See you tomorrow, Jesse,' Sabiha said.

I hustled Sarah into the house. 'I cannot believe you just did that.' I exclaimed as I slammed the door.

'I was helping you. You're playing it so cool she probably doesn't realise you're interested in her at all.'

'That's not true,' I muttered, wondering if it was true. Did Sabiha have any idea I liked her, at all? It was best she didn't. I had to woo her slowly. 'Anyway, I've got it under control. If she doesn't know now, she will soon.' I felt anticipation at her seeing the zombie love story graphic novel. 'And we're now critique buddies.'

'Go, Jesse. You're finally stepping up.' She high-fived me.

I grinned. Yes, it was all coming together nicely.

Chapter 6

Brian and I waited for Sabiha at the bus stop, wearing a denim skirt and tight top. I gulped, admiring how she looked cool and tough. We were catching the bus from St Albans to Highpoint Shopping Centre. She'd told us she was getting out of going to religious classes by her mum, but wouldn't give details. There was a squirrelly energy about her. I didn't ask too many questions. I was just happy to spend time with her.

I'd never cared about what I wore before, but now I tugged at my loose jeans and even looser shirt. Maybe it was time to go shopping.

Brian kissed her on the cheek and yawned. 'It's the break of dawn.'

'It's nine a.m,' she said as she kissed me on the cheek.

I desperately wanted to lean in and kiss her back but was too scared to risk it. I was getting more comfortable in her presence. Since parent-teacher night we'd been sending each other our writing via email. Reading her writing was like seeing into her soul. She'd sent me a story about an orphaned girl whose mother abandoned her daughter to an orphanage to marry a millionaire. There had been such venom and anger in the mother's description and then the daughter's bloody retribution as she burned the millionaire's mansion down with him in it. There had been a moment as the daughter was watching the mansion burning and thinking about her mother burning in the flames, and then it was revealed that her mother was at her feet, safe from the fire.

I knew from the story that Sabiha loved her mother and resented her in equal parts. That something happened that made her feel betrayed. Now I just had to find some way to coax more information about her personal life and who she was.

'Is it too early for you?' Sabiha asked me.

'No, but then I wasn't the one who stayed up half the night watching a Justin Timberlake special.' I glanced at Brian, who was droopily winking.

'Brian!' She whacked him on the shoulder. 'I thought we were going to watch it together.'

The bus arrived, and we walked down the back. I wanted to sit next to Sabiha, but as I was first in the aisle, Brian sat next to me and then Sabiha next to him. We made small talk, for once the conversation flowing. Brian was droopy and leaned his head back, contributing now and then, but Sabiha and I were doing most of the talking, recapping our week at school.

We arrived at Highpoint Shopping Centre, and as we walked in most of the shops were still opening, and the walkways were empty and silent.

'I told you it was barely dawn.' Brian gloated.

'There's Justin.' Sabiha pointed to a shop window.

'Where?' Brian stared around him wildly.

I laughed silently beside her.

'Very funny.' Brian stuck his middle finger in the air and walked off.

I laughed harder, feeling a sense of euphoria and goodwill. This was the first time that we were vibing together so naturally. I didn't feel constrained or shy. I could just be myself. Sabiha laughed even harder, and that set me off. We followed Brian, weaving drunkenly as laughter overcame us.

'Where do you think he went?' Sabiha asked when we reached the escalators. Brian had stomped up them and vanished.

'There's only one thing that will make him more human.' I pointed to the cafe. Sure enough, we found Bran inside, ordering a cappuccino. Sabiha added a hot chocolate to the order, and I got a juice. Brian sat moodily as we waited. When the cappuccino arrived, he looked at it like a lost love.

Sabiha took a sip of her hot chocolate. 'Your hair looks great today.'

'Thanks,' he said grudgingly. 'I've got to go to the loo.'

When he was gone, I made sucking noises.

'Shut up.' She slapped my arm.

My arm tingled where she touched it. I remember I'd brought something for her. 'Before I forget.' I opened my satchel. 'I read the piece you wrote about the Bosnian mosque.'

'You did?' Sabiha crossed her legs.

I fought to drag my eyes back to her face.

'Because there was no rush.'

'There were some great paragraphs.' I pointed to a few lines that I'd ticked in red pen. 'I've also made suggestions.' While I was talking, Brian returned to the table and sipped his cappuccino.

'Thanks, Jesse.' She squeezed my hand. 'That's really helpful.'

I smiled. Joy suffused me. She was effortlessly tactile. Her hand lingered. 'I hope the newspaper likes it too.'

There was a beat as she stared into my eyes. She was looking at me differently. There was something between us. She leaned forward. Was she going to kiss me? She glanced at Brian, who winked.

Sabiha blushed with embarrassment. It was all out in the open. Brian knew we liked each other. My plan was working. It was just a matter of time before things fell into place.

'Here's my story.' I handed her a sheaf of papers.

'I'll read it and get back to you.' She put both stories in my handbag. The rest of the day was a dream. We spent hours browsing shops, Sabiha and I were entranced at the bookshop, and we shared recommendations. It was a perfect day. We caught the bus home together, and I floated. On the way home, we sat in the backseat again. Brian ceded me the middle seat this time, so I was next to Sabiha. We were quieter, tired out from our day. The slanting sun from the window hit us, making us drowsy. Sabiha leaned her head against the headrest and dozed, ending up with her head on my shoulder. I held myself still, smiling as I looked at her. Her hand drifted into my lap, and I held it.

Brian looked over and waggled his eyebrows. When we got off at St Albans train station, Sabiha hugged Brian and then turned to me and hugged me, effortlessly and naturally. I breathed in her hair, feeling the shock of her breasts pressed against me. In the next moment, she was gone with a wave. I smiled widely.

'Look at you Jesse. You're making a move,' Brian said as we walked home.

I glanced at him. 'You don't mind?'

'Sabiha's my best friend. Like you.' He put his arm around my shoulders.

I wanted to ask him if he'd come out to Sabiha, but it wasn't my place to dictate his coming out. He had to do it when he was ready. 'But the two of you flirt like crazy. It's almost like you're together,' I said instead. Even today, they'd been exchanging PDA and flirting.

'We're just both natural extroverts and bring that out in each other. It means nothing.'

I was reassured. I walked like I was bouncing on a cloud. Happiness carrying me home. This was it. This was when we would transition into something more. I couldn't believe it. I wouldn't even need my grand gesture.

On Monday, I walked out of my house, and Brian was sitting on my fence. 'We'll meet Sabiha on the oval today.'

'Oval?' I looked at him questioningly.

'Yeah, Adnan hangs out there in the morning, so I thought we'd join him.'

Something about the way he made that statement gave me pause. He was acting too cool and collected, which set off my spider senses. Brian was hiding something. He clenched his hands on his backpack straps, and glanced at me and away. He was nervous.

'Sounds great,' I said, wondering about this new turn of events but determined not to ask Brian questions. He'd just made the big step of coming out to me. If something else was going on with him, I needed to let him share at his own pace.

Brian and I were waiting for Sabiha at the oval when we saw Adnan walking up. 'Hey, bro.'

Brian and Adnan did this manly handshake thing, holding each other around the arms while I watched on, bemused.

Adnan looked at me. I nodded my head, opting out of the bro shake. Adnan nodded back.

'You seen Sabiha?' Brian asked.

Adnan shook his head. His face changed, and he pointed behind us. I turned to see Sabiha with Gemma and Dina on each side of her. This was a new one. Gemma and Dina usually hung out with us on the oval at lunchtime, but they'd never sought us out in the mornings. This was usually our time.

'There you are!' Brian exclaimed when he saw Sabiha. He gave her a smacking kiss.

I leaned in, kissing her on the cheek, barely making contact but feeling like a million bucks. I did it. I'd broken the physical barrier. We were now kissing friends. Now it was just a matter of time until we became lip-kissing friends.

'Hey cuz.' Adnan kissed her, too.

Dina came over and gave me and Brian pecks. I was so shocked; I stood like a statue. Did Gemma want to be this close to us? I hadn't forgotten how she'd tried to separate Sabiha from us, claiming her like a prize to get next to Adnan.

Dina turned to Adnan and kissed him, holding onto his shoulders and leaning in way too much. Oh, so this was the game again. She wanted to be friends with Sabiha to get with Adnan.

'I want a ciggie,' Gemma whined when the hellos were over.

When we got to the oval, Dina and Gemma pulled out their packets while Brian scabbed a smoke from Adnan.

'I didn't know you smoked,' Sabiha said to Brian.

He eyed the cigarette like he was shocked to find it in his hand. 'I'm more of a social smoker.'

I sniggered. Brian was a chameleon. His only goal was to blend in with everyone around him.

I stood on the edge of the group with Sabiha. We were the only ones who didn't smoke. I loved that about her. That she didn't go with the crowd to fit in, but stood her ground. I knew she was my kind of zombie girl.

'It's just you and me, kid.' I smiled.

'Since we're the only ones who don't think it's fun to suck on a cancer stick.'

'You should try before you judge.' Smoke punctuated Adnan's words. He offered her his packet.

Sabiha pushed it away. 'Thanks, but no thanks.'

'What about you, Jesse?' Adnan offered.

'I've got bronchitis.' It was half true. I'd had it when I was younger, but in adolescence my lungs had strengthened. I just didn't want to smoke. After seeing Mum suffer from a cancer that came out of nowhere, I would not do something stupid that could lead to health issues. I knew what it was like to have your life ruined by illness.

Adnan returned the packet to his shirt pocket.

Sabiha and I moved away from the smokers. 'I read your article.' Sabiha reached into her backpack.

I'd written about teenagers who cared for their ill parents, interviewing my peers at Young Carers Network, an organisation that was funded by the government funded to support those of us who were young carers. Sarah had joined when she was young and now I was a member, too. It was good to talk to people in the same boat as me, forced to grow up too soon and care for their parents. The constant stress and pressure, feeling out of step with our peers.

Sabiha stood closer to me and leaned my story on one of her books so I could go over my notes. I breathed in the scent of her vanilla perfume and had the desire to nuzzle her neck.

'I've only got minimal feedback because it was amazing.'

She met my eyes. We were centimetres apart. All I had to do was lean down slightly. Brian exclaimed from near us, and I knew our friends were close to us. Now was not the time.

'Thanks.' I reached for my story, my hand brushing against hers, and I saw goose-pimples break across her skin. She wasn't immune to me. She was feeling something.

'Where did you get the idea from?' Her brow furrowed with curiosity.

'Someone I know is a carer.' The usual lie tripped off my tongue before I thought about it. I wanted to get to know her and get her to know me, but I still had my guard up. How could I expect her to open herself up to me if I didn't open up to her?

I opened my mouth, wanting to tell the truth, when Brian interrupted. 'Come here, gorgeous.' He hugged Sabiha to his side, planting a smacking kiss on her cheek.

That cock blocker. The rage that suffused me took me by surprise. I was never angry at Brian, but now watching the careless way he was touching her, the way Sabiha blushed and relaxed her body against Brian, bitter jealousy filled me. I wanted nothing more than to rip them apart. Hit Brian. Wipe the smirk off his face. The violent feelings took me by surprise. How could I be feeling like this about my best friend?

I spent the day slightly shell-shocked. Dampening down my feelings.

'What's with you, bro?' Brian asked as we walked home together. 'You've been giving me the silent treatment all day.'

'You noticed, did you?' I muttered.

'Seriously.'

I took a deep breath, working up my courage. 'I don't like the way you have your hands all over Sabiha.'

'Wow, we're just friends.' Brian lifted his hands up in surrender.

'Does she know that?' I demanded.

'What do you mean?' Brian asked.

'I mean, when you're hugging her, it doesn't look like she thinks you're just friends. I think she thinks you're something more.'

Brian smiled. 'Come on, you're taking this too seriously.'

I sped up, rage working through me.

Brian ran to catch up. 'Sorry, I didn't mean to be a jerk. I didn't realise you really fell for her.'

'Yeah, I did. And I think she's feeling something for me, but you keep cockblocking me.' I couldn't believe the words cockblock passed my lips. It was almost too blokey coming out of my mouth. Brian thought so too, because he was looking at me with his mouth formed in an 'oh' of surprise. Our eyes caught, and we laughed.

'Cockblocking. Seriously.' Brian bent forward laughing, and he set me off even more. After the wave passed, he stood, wiping his eyes. 'Sorry, I didn't mean to be a prick. I'll have the "just friends" talk with her tonight and give you more space.'

'Good.' I sighed, feeling better now that everything was out in the open.

'You know, you probably need an opportunity to cross over the line. Some sort of event.' I could see his brain furiously working it over. 'I'll come by later and tell you how the convo went.'

I had dinner with my family and then went to my bedroom to complete my homework, but I couldn't concentrate. I kept glancing at the clock, waiting for Brian to come over and tell me how the conversation went.

I was in my room when Brian barely knocked and slammed the door open.

'Did you talk to Sabiha?' I demanded.

'Yeah, yeah, I had the just friends talk. She knows where we're at. You've got nothing to worry about. The path is completely smooth for you.' He sat on my bed with a bounce.

'Did you come out to her?' I asked, after there was a beat with no more information forthcoming.

'No need. She knows we're friends and nothing more.'

'Are you worried about her accepting you because—' After spending more time with Sabiha, I was now convinced that Brian had nothing to worry about, but he interrupted me.

'No, I just don't want to put that on her at the moment. She's got enough going on with her mum.'

My ears perked up. What was happening with Sabiha's mum? I usually appreciated Brian respecting confidentiality, after all, as I was the number one beneficiary because he never shared my mother's issues with anyone, but this time I had to bite my lip from asking questions and putting him in an awkward spot.

'I'm going to have a party.' Brian opened his notebook and waved a pencil in the air as he spoke.

'What?' It took me a moment to change gears.

'We should have a party at my house. My parents are going away to visit my aunt. Greg and I will have the house to ourselves. I talked to him, and he's up for it.'

Greg was Brian's older brother, and he always looked for an opportunity to throw a party when their parents were away.

'I was thinking of a superhero party! What do you think? This will give you the chance to spend time with Sabiha outside of school and cross over the line.' He looked so eager and excited.

'I guess.' I knew there was more to it than his desire to play matchmaker. He wanted to have a party for a reason of his own. My mind flashed back to the bro-handshake between him and Adnan this morning. Did they linger a moment too long? I pushed the thought away. It wasn't my business.

Brian barely gave me the chance to answer before he got a pen and paper and started writing a to-do list.

I turned back to my computer, thinking about it. Imagining Sabiha in a superhero costume, the lycra tight. Dancing with her. Talking with her. Maybe Brian was right, and this could be my chance.

Chapter 7

The next morning, Brian and I walked to the oval where Adnan was standing on the sideline. Soon after, Dina and Gemma arrived. I kept my eyes on the front, waiting for Sabiha to show. When she finally did, joy suffused me.

'Hello love!' Brian grabbed her into a bear hug, lifting her off the ground. 'Isn't it a beautiful morning?'

As he swung her in his arm, she put her hands on his shoulders, her whole body flush with his. She smiled and leaned into him. Anger burnt through me. He'd just had the "just friends" talk!

Brian met my gaze, and I glared at him. He mimed sorry.

'He's been insufferable,' Dina shouted.

'What's going on?' Sabiha asked after he set her on her feet.

'The party is all set.' Brian handed Sabiha an invitation to attend a comic book character costume party.

I yawned. He'd stayed up late designing the invite, and then I'd typed it up and created graphics before printing them out on my colour printer.

'Who are you coming as?' Brian demanded.

'I don't—'

He cut Sabiha off before she finished. 'Because I'm torn between the Riddler or the Joker.'

'We all know the Riddler is out of your league, Brian,' Dina quipped.

'So you're coming as Poison Ivy?' Brian glared at her. We all laughed. 'What about you, Adnan?' Brian continued.

'He'd be a perfect Superman.' Dina's eyes zeroed in on his chest. Adnan smirked. He thrust his chest and stood in the Superman stance, arms crossed.

'Gemma?' Brian asked as he bummed a ciggie off Adnan.

'Supergirl.' Gemma watched Adnan. Dina's eyes narrowed. Brian coughed on his cigarette smoke. Everyone laughed as he got his breath back.

I watched between Dina and Gemma, wondering how their quest for Adnan woul pan out. I knew how a love triangle could be awkward. Brian looked unperturbed by their drama, and I felt foolish for thinking that he and Adnan were anything more than friends.

'What about Jesse?' Dina asked. 'Who could he be?'

Everyone looked at me. I wanted to squirm under their attention.

'I know.' Brian came to stand behind Jesse and me, putting a hand on our shoulders and pushing us closer together. 'Peter Parker.'

I knew he was trying to apologise for earlier by pushing Sabiha and me closer. I didn't mind.

'He is the perfect Peter Parker.' Dina approached me and looked into my eyes. 'Unassuming, yet has hidden depths.'

What game was she playing? A minute ago, she was flirting with Adnan, yet now she's flirting with me? I knew she wasn't attracted to me. She'd never even glanced in my direction.

I held her gaze, attempting to figure her out.

'That's our Jesse.' Sabiha put her arm around my waist. 'Full of depth.'

I turned and looked at her. Was Sabiha jealous? She was glaring at Dina.

'Maybe I should come as Mary-Jane?' Dina put her hand on my chest, and I looked at her again. 'I'd look good as a redhead.'

There was a smile on Dina's face but no emotion in her eyes. It was like she was play-acting.

'Cat Woman is sexier,' Adnan called out.

Dina backed away. 'Cat Woman it is.' She sashayed back to Adnan and Gemma.

The bell rang, and we headed to class.

I vowed to watch Dina closer in the future. Something was going on with her. She'd been all about Adnan. Or maybe she was just using him to shit-stir Sabiha. The two of them had a weird relationship. They had acted like frenemies for so long and now had an uneasy friendship. It was a question I was determined to ponder further.

***

Sabiha came to school the next day wearing a cap. She looked adorable, peering out from under the brim. I thought nothing of it until our Science teacher, Mr Kumar, commanded her to remove it, and Sabiha asked to keep it on.

Mr Kumar smiled, sensing weakness. He and Sabiha had had a few clashes in the past when she didn't do her homework and didn't show remorse. Her cavalier approach to schooling bemused me. She always seemed to be in her own world, but after parent-teacher night, I had more insight. If her mother had health issues, then she couldn't give Sabiha's academic performance any time.

'Take it off now or go to the principal's office.' Mr Kumar's brows furrowed as he stared her down.

Sabiha removed her cap. Her normally blonde hair was now covered with brown patches. Students around us gasped when they saw her hair. Did she do that on purpose?

'Perhaps if you paid more attention to Science, you would have had a better outcome,' Mr Kumar said, smiling.

'I was aiming for this look.' Sabiha pulled her hair out of her ponytail. With her hair down, it was even more obvious that this was a hair dye disaster. I turned to Brian, who sunk lower into his chair.

'Did you do this?' I asked.

'It's not my fault. She didn't have enough dye.'

I glared at him. Brian should have known better.

Mr Kumar and Sabiha had a verbal spat, and he sent her out of class. Sabiha sauntered out, sashaying her hips and throwing her hair over her shoulder, taunting the class with her multicoloured hair. Where did she get her moxy from? The more someone tried to bring her down, the harder she threw the shade back.

Mr Kumar spoke to her five minutes later in the corridor, and Sabiha returned to the class, looking unchanged and unapologetic. She sat and doodled in her notebook for the rest of the class.

At lunchtime, we sat on the oval, with students walking past and pointing and whispering as they watched Sabiha.

'Maybe you should put your cap on.' Brian handed it to her. She threw it back on the ground.

'I wouldn't be caught dead like that,' Dina pronounced loudly, looking at Sabiha disapprovingly.

I wasn't surprised. Dina was a conformist. Her fashion choices were ordinary and pedestrian, jeans, t-shirts, always tasteful, never flashy. She loved her jewellery, and gold always glittered around her neck and wrists.

'I'm not a wuss,' Sabiha retorted.

Dina's lips flattened with frustration and anger, and she flounced off, Gemma in tow.

'You're so brave.' Brian said. 'I would have faked pneumonia rather than go out like that.'

Sabiha looked disappointed. 'What's the big deal? It's only hair.'

'It's more than that,' Brian got excited. 'Hair expresses our individuality.'

'It's just dead cells,' she said.

She was my perfect zombie girl. She was echoing all my thoughts.

'Perhaps the question is why you don't think it's important?' I asked, seizing the opportunity to find out more about her.

'When you have a mum like mine, public embarrassment is a waste of emotion. When she's sick, she can be like a kid, and when she's healthy, she's not much better, so I don't find this shit,' she waved her hand at the school, 'important. I only care what people I respect think about me.'

I knew her mother had health issues, but she'd never specified, and I'd never asked. If I did, I'd have to tell her about my mum, and I wasn't ready for that. She'd told me her mother had nervous breakdowns, but now I knew it was more than that. She was exactly like me. Our eyes locked and I couldn't look away.

'You really don't care if other people like you or not...' Brian sounded incredulous.

'Not if I don't like them,' she said.

I believed her. She was completely fearless about other people's opinions. She was so brave, so much braver than me. I was still hiding. Still keeping my mother a dirty secret from her and her from everyone else. I envied her.

Brian glanced at the buildings behind us. 'We're different.' There was such a naked look of longing on his face. 'I'd give anything for people to think I'm cool, but they know I'm a loser.'

That was one reason Brian and I were best friends. We kept ourselves hidden, only showing our peers what we wanted them to see.

'You are cool,' Sabiha blurted. She glanced at me before continuing. 'You dress nicely, and your hair is always perfect.'

Brian smiled sadly. 'No, you're cool, Sabiha. Because you don't give a shit about what those idiots think of you.' He walked away.

'But—' she protested.

'Leave him.' I held her arm. 'He needs to be alone.'

'I didn't want to make him feel bad.'

'He does that himself.' I knew he needed a time-out to process. 'He's right, you know,' I finally said.

'About what?'

'You are cool.' My heart skipped a beat. I loved her. I loved Sabiha. She was everything I'd ever wanted, and now I knew I was right in thinking we belonged together. We were alike.

'Thanks,' her voice was a whisper.

I dipped my head, wanting to kiss her. The moment was perfect.

She blushed. 'The bell's about to go.' She jumped off the table and bent to get her backpack, hiding her face. After what seemed like forever, the bell rang.

I suddenly felt so powerful. She was blushing and awkward in my presence. Gone was the self-confident Sabiha who made me feel out of depth. The foot was now on the other foot. I loved being the one who wasn't freaking out. I jumped up too, and stood so that we were almost touching. We stared at each other. 'Saved by the bell,' I said.

She bit her lip. Her heartbeat pulsed in her throat.

'We'd better go, or we'll be late.' Her voice was tight.

I stepped aside and let her lead. As we walked to English class side by side, our arms almost touched as we walked. I resisted the urge to take her hand.

She stopped in front of the toilets. 'I'll meet you in class.'

I walked to class feeling a million bucks. My plan was working.

***

Sabiha walked in as Ms Partridge was writing on the board. I expected Ms Partridge to tell her off for being late, but she smiled and finished writing the learning intention on the board before turning to speak to the class. 'As you all know, the *St Albans News* has been running a weekly feature publishing articles from each school in the district. It is with great pleasure I congratulate two of our very own students, Sabiha Omerović and Jesse James.' The class clapped as Ms Partridge handed us a copy of the newspaper.

Sabiha flipped through the paper and found our articles on page thirteen. I peered over her shoulder at our two bylines side-by-side, an omen of things to come. James and Omerović side by side.

'We did it!' she exclaimed. She turned to me with a smile of joy and hugged me, her hands moving to my back.

I moved my hands to her waist and pulled her against me. She gasped as she met my gaze. 'Congratulations.' I leaned down and brushed my lips against her cheek, resisting the urge to kiss her. I was aware of the eyes of our peers in the classroom.

'To you too,' she whispered, letting go.

I slowly moved my hands from her waist, a lingering caress through her t-shirt, gratified to feel her shiver. I spent the rest of the class in a daze, one part of me still copying notes from the board, the other part fantasising about kissing Sabiha. It was just a matter of time. I caught her stealing glances at me. When I met her gaze, her cheeks flushed, and she looked away self-consciously. I bit back a smile.

After class, students congratulating me surrounded me. Sabiha was next to me, and then suddenly, she was in the doorway. I looked at her and smiled. She smiled back weakly and left the classroom. I looked for her after school, but she'd already left the school grounds, probably excited to show off to her family.

Brian sent me a message that he was meeting someone after school, so I speed-walked home by myself.

When I got home, Mum was in the living room watching television. 'Look mum. I won a newspaper competition.'

I handed Mum the article and her glasses. She read it, and tears glistened on her cheeks. The article was about young carers that Sabiha had proofread for me.

'I am so proud of you.' Mum kissed me on the cheek and hugged the newspaper to her chest.

Marian came in, and Mum showed her the article. Marian read it as Mum held onto the newspaper. She smiled softly at me. 'You're so talented, Jesse. Your writing is helping to change the world.'

The two of them laughed and spoke for a few minutes before Marian took her leave.

'Jesse, hand me the phone,' Mum asked after I'd walked Marian out.

'Who are you calling?' I asked as I handed her the phone.

Mum cracked open the phone book. 'Everyone, silly.'

I laughed and left her to it, her eyes sparkling and her cheeks flushed with happiness. I walked into the kitchen. Marian had cleaned, and she'd prepared a casserole that was bubbling on the stovetop.

I went to my room, trying to concentrate on my homework, but gave it up and worked on the zombie love story. While my frantic energy to make a big gesture had abated, winning the competition had ignited my muse. I'd been working on the graphic novel for Sabiha, but now I thought larger. Charlie and I were nearing the end of our first draft, and I was really proud of the story. Charlie's illustrations were mind-blowing with detail. Maybe we could get our graphic novel published. I researched publication opportunities and lost track of time.

The door slammed open, and I heard the murmur of voices as Sarah and Mum spoke. I left my bedroom and saw Sarah reading the article as she stood in the hallway.

'Jesse, this is amazing.' She gasped when she finished, grabbing me in a tight hug.

'We need to have cake,' Mum told Sarah.

'I'll go to the cheesecake shop and buy it.' Sarah got her keys.

'Don't worry about it. I need nothing,' I insisted. Sarah had just returned from work and was exhausted. She didn't need to run another errand.

'I won't be long.' Sarah left, still in her dirty scrubs.

I laid out plates for dinner and turned off the casserole, eavesdropping as Mum continued her phone calls. She was now talking to my paternal aunt, working her way alphabetically through the address book. I returned to my room and worked on my zombie novel. A little while later, I heard the front door slam and expected Sarah to call me, but she didn't. Maybe she was having a shower first. I zoned out.

There was a soft knock on the door, and Sarah peered in. 'Come to the kitchen.'

I nodded, quickly hitting save before I stood and followed. Sarah had set the table with a cake with balloons hanging off the chairs. Sarah had bought a picture frame too, and framed my newspaper article in it, so it was sitting on the table. There was a chocolate plaque stating congratulations on it.

'We're so proud of you,' Sarah said as I sat.

My eyes watered. 'It's just a newspaper article.'

'No, it's not. It's a realisation of your dream. You're a writer.'

I sat straighter. This was true. Mum was smiling at me, her eyes glassy and glowing.

'You take after your father,' she whispered. 'He was a writer, too. He wrote me the most beautiful love letters. I'll leave them to you in my will, and you can read them then. They were very risque.' She fanned herself.

Sarah and I laughed. I loved hearing about my father. He'd died when I was young, and Mum hadn't spoken about him for the longest time. I knew he'd loved reading, and I'd inherited his library. Some of my most prized books came from him, the dog-eared copies of *1984*, *All is Quiet on the Western Front*, *The Call of the Wild*. When I'd read his books and then the notations on the margin, it was like I was bringing him back to life again.

Sarah had a shower while I served. After the cake, Sarah took Mum for a shower and then helped her to bed. I washed the dishes and walked to my room. Mum was lying in bed, the bedside lamp on. Beside it was my framed article, and she was gazing at it. She turned and, seeing me in the doorway, waved me over.

I lay on the bed next to her, curling my arm around her waist and laying my head next to hers on the pillow.

'I worry that I'm a burden on you and Sarah.' Mum stared up at the ceiling. 'You both have to sacrifice so much to care for me.'

'It's not a sacrifice. It's what you do for family.' I clasped my hand in hers. 'Anyway, things are so much easier now with Marian.'

'I know, but I don't want you to be held back in life because you're taking care of me. I want you to go to university and achieve your dreams. Maybe I should go to a nursing home. There are people to care for me there, and the two of you would be free.'

'Don't you dare say that.' I gripped her arm hard and leaned on my elbow to look down at her. 'You're the one that holds us together. Without you, Sarah and I would drift away. We need you. Promise you won't ever say that again.'

Mum looked at me and caressed my cheek. 'My dear Jesse. You have such a big heart.' She patted my hand. 'Okay. I promise.'

I kissed her on the cheek and stood, turning off the lamp. 'Love you Mama.'

'Love you Jesse.'

I closed the bedroom door behind me. Sarah was in the kitchen, making her lunch for the next day.

'What's with the sad face? This is a day for celebrating,' she said jovially.

'Mum said she should go to a nursing home.'

Sarah put her salad in the fridge. 'I hope you told her she was being ridiculous.'

'Yes, I did. You don't think she'll do it?'

'She can't do it if we don't let her. But there is something you can do to make her feel better.'

'What?' I asked.

'Plan your future. She worries, thinks she's holding you back from thinking about what you'll do after high school and that you won't go to university.'

It was true. I was too scared to think about the future. I tied my whole life up with caring for Mum and pushed away anything that would jeopardise that.

I nodded. 'Okay. I'm going to make some plans.'

'Love you, baby bro.' Sarah kissed me on the forehead, and I followed her down the hall.

I'd already started researching how to submit our graphic novel. Now I had another reason to actually go ahead with it. I needed my mother to know that I was going to be alright. That she was not a burden in my life, but a source of inspiration.

Chapter 8

'Did you hear the news?' Brian demanded as I walked out my front door.

'What news?' I shrugged on my backpack and stepped in with him, feeling distracted and dazed. I'd had to pierce another hole in my belt that morning as my weight training was having an effect. When I'd looked at myself in the mirror, I'd felt wonder. My biceps were getting more defined and torso looking taut. When I put on my t-shirt and jeans, it hid all my gains, and I was happy with that. I wasn't ready to show off my new look.

'Adnan won a car on *The Price is Right*.' Brian's voice was high-pitched, and he was bouncing as he walked.

'Good for him.'

'I know. Can you believe someone we know has a car? I wonder if he'll drive us somewhere.'

'Why would he?' Adnan did not strike me as the altruistic type.

'He is Sabiha's cousin. He'll drive her, surely.'

'I don't think so.' Adnan didn't treat Sabiha like a beloved relative, more like a pest.

'We don't know that,' Brian said.

I stopped trying to break his delusions and let him prattle on with his imaginings. He walked quickly, and I had to quicken my pace to keep up with him.

At school the next day, Sabiha was standing next to Adnan as I walked up. She wasn't wearing a cap anymore, instead, her hair was tied in a ponytail, the patches visible here and there. A group surrounded Adnan while Sabiha stared moodily at him.

'They taped it a month ago, and I was waiting for the episode to air,' Adnan explained.

'You were so lucky.' Dina watched him with worshipful eyes.

'Luck had nothing to do with it,' Adnan said. 'I went three times before they picked me to appear as a contestant. It took me that long to figure out how the system works.'

'What system?' Brian asked.

'They want people who have an interesting story. I told them I was an orphan once, but I think that was too sad for them, so I pulled back a bit.'

'You deceived people,' Sabiha said.

Adnan lifted an eyebrow. 'I gave people a story they wanted to hear.'

I admired his gumption. He'd learnt how to work the system. That's what one needed to survive—a good story; something for me to keep in mind.

Others approached. I saw Sabiha grab her backpack and leave. I called her name and ran after her. 'Was your mum happy about the article?'

'For a whole five seconds, until Adnan, the movie star, made his debut appearance.'

I winced, seeing the bitterness on her face. She'd been so excited about the article. I got the sense her family didn't really give her enough attention. I knew what it was like when you had a sick mother. You always played second best. At least my mother and Sarah made a big deal about me.

'They're all hoping they're getting a ride from him.' I glanced over my shoulder, and so did she. The crowd grew. 'Once they realise there's nothing in it for them, they'll back off. There's no way Adnan will spoil his car with that rabble in it.'

'Was your family happy about the article?'

'My sister got me a cake. It was all right.' I underplayed my night, not wanting to make her feel bad.

'That's so kind.' Her voice was high-pitched, sounding as if she was close to tears.

'There's light at the end of the tunnel.' I kept my voice neutral.

'What?' She side-eyed me.

'No one will talk about your hair anymore.'

Sabiha laughed, her tears drying up. Happiness punched me in the gut. I did that. I made her feel good.

At lunchtime, Brian tugged us toward the oval.

'I'm not in the mood to be Adnan's fan club today.' Sabiha turned away. 'Let's go to the library.'

'Come on, don't be a sour loser,' Brian urged.

'I'm not a sour loser. I just don't want to be around him. Let's go to the library.'

'I'll meet you there.' Brian walked off briskly.

'Prick!' Sabiha muttered under her breath. She looked at me, but I pretended I didn't hear. She and Brian had their own friendship.

'I've got a better spot.' I led her to my favourite reading spot, under the elm tree in front of the carpark.

'It's beautiful.' Sabiha looked up at the branches curving like a canopy. They were so long that they draped on the ground, creating a privacy curtain.

There were a few students under the shaded area. I sat next to the trunk and laid down my jacket for Sabiha to sit on.

'You don't need to do that.' She bent and went to lift it.

'Yes, I do. You want to keep your skirt clean.'

'I'll only sit if we share.' She spread it and sat, patting it next to her.

I was rapt. As I sat, we pressed up against each other.

'What are you writing at the moment?' Sabiha asked.

'I'm working on a graphic novel with my mate, Charlie. He's doing the drawings and I'm writing it.' I'd been planning on talking to him about seeking publication and had collected my research, but that would have to wait.

'Sounds great. Tell me more.'

I opened my mouth but didn't know what to say. I couldn't tell her the storyline, or she'd know. 'It's a zombie book. It's still early days, and we're figuring out the storyline.'

'I'd love to help and critique when you're ready to show it to someone.'

I nodded. I knew she'd have to read it at some point. After all, she was the inspiration for me writing it, but the thought made my stomach flutter with butterflies. What if, after all my work and effort, she didn't like it?

'Why is this the first time it's been only the two of us?' Sabiha mused, breaking me out of my anxiety spiral.

I carefully peeled back the Gladwrap from the other half of my sandwich. 'I got the feeling that you wanted to be alone with Brian.' I decided to be honest and see where the chips landed.

She winced. 'Brian and I are just friends.' She put her sandwich down and placed her hand on my arm. 'Nothing more.'

'Really.' I stared at her hand, my skin tingling. She went to remove it, but I put my hand over it and held it. 'I'm glad to hear that.'

I wanted desperately to kiss her. This was finally my moment. There was no one around, no one to interrupt or cockblock.

'I want us all to be friends.' Her hand tensed under mine, her cheeks pinking.

I met her gaze and saw trepidation there. It wasn't the right moment. She wasn't ready.

I smiled and patted her hand, and let go. 'We're friends.' I was content to wait. Things were finally moving in the right direction.

'What character are you going to be at Brian's party?'

I frowned. 'I don't know.'

'What about Zorro?'

'Maybe. I've heard that cowboys always get the girl,' I smiled. She laughed again.

We spent the rest of lunch chit-chatting about the party and our favourite reads. I was disappointed when the bell went and I had to give up being with her alone.

I remained at the gym and did weight training after school. Brian was sporadic in his routine, and I'd made it my goal to go at least three times a week. Now that I'd seen there was a definite effect, I hit the weights with renewed enthusiasm.

Afterwards, I walked to Charlie's house. His mum greeted me enthusiastically and led me down the hallway. As I walked past the living room, I heard his three younger siblings shouting as they played a computer game. Charlie's mum knocked and then cracked the door, poking her hand in while she remained in the hallway and flicking the light switch. Charlie opened the door a few seconds later, headphones firmly clamped on his head. He saw me and nodded, moving away to let me enter.

When I closed the door, he removed his headphones and winced as one of his siblings screeched loudly. He flicked on his computer, and white sound filled the room, the monotonous shushing like calming background music for him.

I greeted him and sat on his bed.

'I'm working on the latest illustrations.' He handed me his sketchbook.

I'd recreated the scene with Sabiha's ruined dye job in the zombie world, with Jasper attempting to do a makeover to make him look like a human, and therefore more like Saphire, as she's a zombie who thinks she's a human. When the makeover fails, Saphire comforts him, telling him she accepts him exactly as he is and that everyone is a little bit of a monster inside. He had recreated their near kiss, with Saphire showing uncertainty for the first time as her feelings change for him. Charlie had perfectly captured Sabiha's vulnerability; her eyes were wide, her lips parted, and my skin raised in goosebumps.

'This is amazing.' I gently caressed Saphire/Sabiha. 'Did you read my email?' I'd emailed Charlie the research I'd found about a literary speed dating event at the Quill & Quire Collective writing organisation.

Charlie nodded.

'Do you want us to submit the graphic novel?'

Charlie nodded again.

'Great.' I smiled with relief. 'Let's work on the pitch.'

'You do it. You'll have to pitch by yourself.' His face was impassive, and his voice held no emotion. Most people would assume he was unbothered by the thought of letting me submit by myself and take the limelight, but just because Charlie didn't show any emotion, it didn't mean he didn't feel. I knew he felt everything, and he felt it deeply.

'No. We did this together and will pitch together, or we don't do it all.'

Charlie glanced up, his eyelashes wet. 'I can't.' Charlie gestured to his headphones and the white noise. The speed dating was all in one room, with participants moving around and taking turns pitching to participating publishers. The atmosphere would be loud and echoey, an impenetrable nightmare of noise that would set off Charlie's anxiety and make him hyperventilate.

'Yes, you can. You just need the right support, and I'm going to make sure you get it.'

Charlie examined my face, attempting to deduce the strength of my resolve.

'I've never lied to you, Charlie, and I'm not now. I promise I'll find a way for us both to pitch publishers at that literary speed dating.' I wanted to reach out and take his hand, comfort him through physical touch, but that's not how Charlie dealt with things.

Charlie reached out, and I handed him his sketchbook. His hand briefly clasped mine and then was gone. Joy filled me. He was on board. Now I had to ensure that Quill & Quire Collective did their part in accommodating Charlie's needs.

Trepidation grazed my skin like an icy breeze. I hoped I wasn't inadvertently lying to Charlie.

We started planning our pitch for the event, brainstorming ideas back and forth that Charlie typed into a Google document we both had access to. By the end of the hour, I was satisfied with our progress. We were on track.

The next day I walked to school with a sprig in my step. Today was the day I was going to tell Sabiha about the book. She was waiting for Brian at the front of the school. My shoelace was undone, so I stopped to tie it. Brian continued. I followed, admiring Sabiha's dark brown hair. She looked beautiful with her green eyes standing out more.

Brian was looking at his phone as I arrived. I heard them talking about movies, mentioning titles like Juno, American Gangster and The Bourne movie.

I got to the table. 'Are you going to the movies?' I dropped my library bag on the ground.

Sabiha signalled Brian. 'We don't know yet.'

Brian shifted, still looking at his phone. 'We're staking out Sabiha's new crush.'

New crush. Sabiha had a new crush. I felt like a ton of bricks landed on top of me, and had to blink rapidly as I processed. I thought we were on the same page, that she liked me and I liked her. We'd had a near kiss on Friday and now she was already crushing on some new guy. When the hell had this happened?

'You want to come?' Brian was still scanning the sessions on his phone. 'We're seeing *The Bourne Supremacy*. You can help provide a cover for us.'

'No, I've seen it. ' I lied, turning and walking away. I needed to get away from both of them. How could Brian not have told me what was going on? I got my emotions under control and waited at the lockers.

Brian arrived, opened his locker door and looked at himself in the mirror.

'Why didn't you tell me?' I demanded, slamming my locker shut so it reverberated loudly.

'Tell you what?' Brian looked at me in surprise.

'That Sabiha had a new crush.'

'You know what she's like. There's a new guy this week and someone else the following week.'

'But we were vibing together.' Maybe I had imagined it? I thought we'd had a connection, that she wanted me to kiss her. What if I was wrong?

'You probably were.' Brian clapped his hand on my shoulder. 'But you know what she's like. As soon as a guy is too into her, she freezes up. Acts all freaked out.'

'You mean I freaked her out because I liked her?' I demanded. What sort of game was she playing?

'Probably.' Brian shrugged.

There was something weird here. Why did she freeze up when a guy liked her? 'What should I do?'

'You either talk it out with her, and that might lead to her saying she's not into you because she's too freaked out, or you could play hard to get.'

'What does that mean?'

'That means don't show her you're into her anymore. Act cold and let her come to you. That's what I would do.' Brian closed his locker.

I followed suit, both of us carrying our textbooks and notebooks as we walked to class. 'Who is he?'

'A hairdresser. Some pretty boy who is Bosnian.' He sat in his seat. 'I don't know if she really likes him, or is just trying him out to bond with her mother.'

'Why does her mother care?' I frowned. I know that Sabiha and her mother were experiencing some sort of tension, with her mum wanting her to go to religious school and do housework, but I didn't realise that their friendship was so fraught that Sabiha would take extreme measures to bond.

'Her mother wants her to be with a Bosnian. It's a whole thing.'

'So Sabiha can't have a boyfriend who isn't Bosnian?' I asked, a sinking feeling in my stomach. If this was the case, then I didn't stand a chance.

Brian shrugged. 'It's a whole ethnic thing.'

It slightly mollified me. If her mother wouldn't let her date outside of her community and Sabiha wanted to get her mother's approval, then this could be the reason. Maybe this wasn't a rejection of me? I had to wait and see what happened. And talk to Sabiha.

I read at lunchtime on the oval, watching Sabiha as she spoke to her friends. She caught me looking at her and looked guilty. I felt better. She knew that there had been something more between us. That we weren't just friends. She hid behind Adnan when she caught me looking at her. Good, she wasn't so indifferent. She felt guilty.

I had to wait until English in session six. Sabiha and I sat at the back in our usual spot. I was getting ready to launch into my questions, but she pre-empted me. 'You coming to the library tomorrow with me and Brian?'

I nodded dazedly. She acted like nothing had happened between us last week, no near kiss, no moment.

'Good. I need you to help me with some recs. You know Brian is useless. I'm so glad I have a friend who shares my love of books.' She emphasised the word friend.

'Is that what we are?' I asked softly. 'Just friends.' I gazed into her eyes, forcing her to look at me.

She met my gaze and quickly glanced away. 'Of course.' She smiled and turned to the board, copying notes from the board.

I watched her for the rest of the session, brooding. When we paired up to share answers to the teacher's questions, she was matter-of-fact and nonchalant, as if she was unbothered, but I noticed her hands were clenched on her pen, her writing thick and black as she pressed heavily into the page. A flicker of hope lit within me.

Sabiha, Brian, and I set off for the library after school the next day. We were walking toward the station when a car slowed to a crawl and followed us. The window rolled down, and Adnan's face appeared. He pushed his sunglasses down his nose. 'Want a lift?'

'Sweet ride,' Brian shouted as he admired Adnan's car from *The Price is Right*.

Adnan nodded smugly.

Brian jumped into the passenger seat and caressed the dashboard. 'This is sick, mate.'

I opened the back door for Sabiha. 'Thanks,' she muttered as I slid across the backseat.

After I got in, Adnan took off. 'Where to?'

'Sunshine library,' Brian said.

Adnan turned onto St Albans Road. 'You'll have to give me directions.'

While Adnan and Brian talked in the front, I stared out the window, trying to think of something to say.

'Here we go.' Adnan screeched to a halt. 'It's a shame you're busy, Brian,' he said as we got out of the car. 'I'm hooking up with my Bosnian mates for a soccer game at Footscray footy ground. We could use your ball skills.'

Brian pulled his leg back inside and closed the door. 'You don't mind, do you?' he yelled through the open window.

Sabiha and I stood on the footpath and watched as Adnan drove off, Brian's arm waving out the side. I waited for Sabiha to turn to me and head for the library, but she forlornly stared down the street.

'I don't think he's coming back.'

'I can't believe he did that,' she whispered.

'That's Brian for you,' I said wryly. 'Always on the lookout for something better.'

We strolled through the library, looking for books and filling our library bags. I watched her through the shelf. She looked miserable. She really was uncomfortable being around me. It made me feel better. I preferred anything other than indifference.

Afterwards, we walked to the station. 'What did you get?' she asked, filling the silence.

'The usual.' I hitched my backpack higher on his shoulder. 'What's the name of your new crush?' I fought to keep my expression neutral so she wouldn't think I was anything more than an interested friend.

'His name is Edo.'

'I hope it works out on Saturday,' I kept my voice even. She glanced at me in surprise, but I stared straight ahead. 'Did you do your English homework? I still have some writing to do.'

'Not yet.' She furrowed her brow.

'I focused on the theme of perception within *To Kill a Mockingbird*.' I rattled on about my essay, enjoying her petulant face. Maybe this was working, and it bothered her that I wasn't bothered about her crush. Way to go Jesse, you're killing it! Maybe Brian's advice was sound, and I had to act cool.

When the train pulled up at St Albans, she mumbled a quick goodbye and leaped out as soon as the doors opened. I followed more slowly. She was almost at the gates when a guy wearing a black leather jacket and ponytail called her name. What a try-hard!

Sabiha turned back to talk to him. As I approached, his mates came up. He started talking to them and walked away from Sabiha without saying goodbye. Shit, shit! It was too late for me to hide. Sabiha turned and met my gaze. She looked on the verge of tears. I'd never seen her so vulnerable. I wanted to hug her. I wanted to punch Edo in the mouth. I did neither.

'You forgot it.' I held up my arm where I'd folded her jacket across.

'Thanks.' Her throat was thick as she took the jacket from me.

'You okay?' I asked.

She was clenching her teeth, fighting so hard to stop crying. 'Sure,' she forced out, angry and breathless.

I handed her a tissue.

She met my eyes, looking angry and vulnerable. 'Thank you.'

'I'll see you at school.' I walked off, leaving her to process. I tried not to walk with a spring in my step. Edo was toast. I was sorry that Sabiha was hurt but also strangely happy. I felt guilty for being happy that she knew what it was like to get blown off so quickly. Karma was a bitch.

Chapter 9

On Monday morning at school, Brian and I were waiting when Sabiha arrived at the oval. Her face was pale, and there were dark circles under her eyes. Was she sick?

'Hello, Miss Sunshine,' Brian sang, buzzing like a battery-powered appliance. 'It's only six days to my paaar-ty!'

'Yeah, I know.' Sabiha sounded flat.

Usually Brian's joy made her smile. Now she looked at him blankly.

'Geez, did someone die?' Brian asked.

'I've got stuff going on. Can we talk tonight?' Her gaze was pleading as she spoke to Brian.

My gaze sharpened. Was this about Edo? Was she still going on about that loser?

Brian frowned. 'I'm not sure...' He was distracted now, waving to Adnan, and then he walked off.

As usual, Brian had missed the signs. He was so involved in himself. Sabiha looked like she was about to cry.

'Sabiha, are you all right?' I asked.

Sabiha let out a muffled sob before quickly turning away and running. I looked around for Brian's help, but he was running around on the oval with Adnan, completely oblivious. It was up to me. I ran after her. She disappeared around the Arts class blocks. I heard her before I saw her. She was crying in deep, heart-wrenching sobs that tugged at my heart. I dropped her backpack at her feet and took her arms, pulling her into a hug.

'It will be all right,' I murmured, rubbing her back. With a long hug and comforting words, I soothed her the way my mother had soothed me.

She leaned back, looking up at me, her cheeks flushed pink, her eyes glistening. She looked so vulnerable and sweet. I'd never seen this softer side of Sabiha. She was usually so tough. I brushed her hair behind her ear before wiping a tear from under her eye. 'Tell me what's wrong.' I reached into my pocket and passed her a hankie.

'I'm going to jail,' she wailed as she blew into my hankie.

'What the...? Start from the beginning,' I commanded.

Sabiha told me that the Twins who had bashed her were cousins of her former friend Shelley. Shelley had talked them into attacking Sabiha because they were having a toxic threesome with their friend Kathleen. When Shelley confessed to the bashing, Sabiha lost it and attacked her.

'I don't even remember doing it. Just this red rage came over me. I wanted to hurt her like she hurt me. I punched her, and she fell to the ground, and then I kicked her again and again. She was gasping on the ground and struggling for breath, and that's when I came back to my body. I ran away, and when I did, I hit something under my foot. It was only when I got to the train station I realised I'd hit her inhaler. I thought maybe I'd killed her, so I called Kathleen's house and pretended to be Shelley's sister. She's alive. I didn't kill her. But now she could get the police onto me. They could arrest me and then my mum. She won't survive this. She'll end up in hospital for sure,' Sabiha wailed, her hand clenched on my hanky as she dabbed at her tears.

I paused a moment, processing what she'd told me. 'I don't think you have anything to worry about.'

'Haven't you listened to what I just told you?'

'Sabiha.' I put my hands on her shoulders, forcing her to look at me. 'If she goes to the police, then it will come out that her cousins bashed *you*.'

'Oh...'

'See...' I stroked her arm. 'I told you everything would be all right.'

She shook her head. 'No, it's not' She broke eye contact. 'My Mum's getting sick again.' She was on the edge of tears again.

I reached over and took her hand in mine. 'What's wrong with your Mum?' This was the question I'd wanted to ask for months, and now I finally had an in.

'Mum suffers from nervous breakdowns. She constantly gets sick. If she doesn't take her medication, she gets sick. She just completely loses touch with reality. She thinks she's talking to movie stars or the president. That she has special powers, and then she goes to hospital and my whole life is stuffed. I end up going to a foster home or to live with strangers.'

As she spoke, I felt goose-pimples. I'd gone through the same thing when Mum was sick with cancer. Worrying about what would happen if she didn't come out of the hospital. Having to stay with my aunt when she was in hospital for surgery and recovering. Strangers trooping in and out of the house. The constant stress of not knowing what tomorrow would bring. The only safe place was school, where there was a reprieve with routine. I knew that Sabiha and I were kindred spirits. Trauma bonded us, and now I finally had my confirmation.

The bell rang. 'Are you okay to go to class?' I picked up her backpack and handed it to her.

She nodded. On the way to the lockers, she ducked into the toilets, returning with her face slightly damp and the redness subsiding from her eyes. We had sessions one and two English, and she was unfocused, gazing out the window with a faraway look. I copied notes and ran interference when the teacher asked us questions.

When the bell rang for recess, I walked Sabiha to her locker, and Brian followed. After we swapped our books, I took her arm and led her down the corridor. 'Aren't you coming to the oval?' Brian asked.

'Not today,' I said, without breaking my stride.

We sat under the elm tree and she told me the rest of her drama. About her grandfather not understanding her mother's illness and believing that prayers would be a magic cure. About her mother's boyfriend, who she didn't like. Sabiha talked and talked, her body unfurling as she released her tension and stress.

'I'll see you in history,' I said as we went our separate ways for third period.

I had biology with Brian, who demanded, 'What's going on with you and Sabiha?'

'Nothing.' I shrugged.

'Are you sure? Looks like she's finally given in. My advice worked, huh?' He smiled archly, looking smug.

'No, she's just having a bad day.' I didn't want to tell him. If he wanted to know what was happening with Sabiha, he should ask her. I wasn't the Sabiha telegram that would share all her business.

'She's always having a bad day.' He waved a hand dismissively.

I was angry on Sabiha's behalf. Brian was minimising the issue because it suited him. The teacher began speaking from the front, and I ignored him for the rest of the lesson. When I met Sabiha in history, she was still pale and distracted.

We all ambled to the oval at lunchtime, but our huddle was out of whack.

'What's with you and Jesse?' Brian asked Sabiha as I walked behind them.

'He's being a friend.'

'Looks to me like he's more than a friend.' His tone was snide. His eyes shifted, and he followed Adnan as he approached.

'Not that you'd know what a friend acted like.' Sabiha's voice was full of sarcasm.

'What do you mean?' Now Brian was defensive.

'Maybe if you stopped being so impressed with Adnan, you'd know,' she snapped. Brian looked shocked. She moved away from Brian and went to stand by me.

Brian pivoted on his heel and left to play with Adnan.

I sat next to Sabiha on the edge of the group. She looked emotionally exhausted. She took out her book and began reading. I knew what it was like; she was overwhelmed with emotion and needed a reprieve from life. I did the same. We read as everyone else talked around us. A little while later, she lay on the grass, and soon her eyes closed, and she dropped the book by her side. I shifted closer so my body gave her shade on her face. She curled against me, her hand clasping mine. I smiled as I continued reading, feeling content. Even though she may not know it consciously, we were definitely on the more than friends track. I watched Brian as he ran joyfully around the oval, his eyes tracing the ball and Adnan in equal measure. I was going to have to talk to him.

The bell rang, and Sabiha droopily opened her eyes, smiling as she saw me peering down at her. 'Time to go to class.' I stood and gently tugged her to her feet, wanting to keep holding her hand but letting it drop instead. We walked to class together, our shoulders touching, and I was content to be back in her orbit.

After school, I waited for Brian at the lockers.

'We need to talk about Sabiha.'

'Sorry, can't. I'm going to play soccer with Adnan.' Brian threw his backpack in and locked the door with a slam. 'See ya.' He ran down the steps at breakneck speed.

I followed leisurely and saw him jumping into Adnan's car before they sped off. An internal alarm bell pinged. Brian and Adnan weren't just friends. 'Oh, Brian, what have you gotten yourself into now?' I murmured under my breath.

I could only deal with one problem at a time. I turned toward home, determined to get Sabiha's help.

***

'I wanted your advice,' I asked Sarah as I handed her the mashed potatoes during dinner. 'My friend's mother suffers from nervous breakdowns.'

Sarah frowned. 'That's not a medical diagnosis.' She scooped the potatoes next to the lamb cutlets.

'Yes, that's what I came with in my research. They're from a Non-English speaking background, and so I think they used the wrong term for her mental illness' I'd searched the term nervous breakdown and found vague explanations about someone struggling with their day-to-day and being unable to function in everyday life. Sabiha's description of her mother's symptoms did not match.

'Okay. What are the symptoms?' Sarah scooped steamed veggies on her plate and passed me the bowl.

'She goes through these phases of hyperactivity. She stays up late cleaning the house over and over and doesn't sleep for days at a time. Then she gets very impulsive, spends money, gives away belongings, forgets to pay bills.'

'Any physical changes?' Sarah swirled her mashed potatoes and veggies together before taking a bite.

'Her eyes glitter and the pupils shrink. She gets itchy and scratches her body and struggles to talk, slurring her words and sounding drunk.'

'Are there auditory hallucinations? She hears voices that tell her to do things?'

I shook my head. 'She imagines things. Thinks she has powers but doesn't hear people talking to her.'

'That's good. If there were auditory hallucinations, it might be Schizophrenia, but all the other symptoms sound more like Bipolar disorder. Does she go through depression?'

'Yes, when the medication hits. She can't move and just lies on the couch.' I remembered Sabiha telling me the way her mother looked. She gave up on life, lying listless and limp on the couch. It brought back flashbacks to Mum's cancer when she couldn't move and just lay there as if she was slowly dying.

'Yes, bipolar is characterised by manic moods and depressive lows. I know where we can get some information for your friend.'

Mum had listened to our conversation without speaking. 'Is it your friend, Sabiha?'

I nodded reluctantly, feeling weird about breaking Sabiha's privacy. I glanced at Sarah. She was unsurprised. She'd probably assumed we were talking about Sabiha but didn't ask.

'You and Sabiha have a lot in common.' Mum patted my hand. 'I'm glad that you have each other. It's tough dealing with such gigantic problems without a friend.'

'Thanks Mum.' She was right. These were the sort of situations that helped to have a friend who empathised. When I'd been going through Mum's illness, Brian was there for me every day. He'd shown such empathy in coming over every day and offering a distraction with us playing a video game or just hanging out with me and lying on the bed as we listened to music. It was out of character for him to be so oblivious to Sabiha. I needed to bring him back into the fold.

After I'd washed the dishes, Sarah and I went to the computer. She showed me the Black Dog Institute website, and we downloaded fact sheets about Bipolar.

***

The next day, I waited for Sabiha by the bike rack. 'I talked to my sister about your mum.'

'Why?' she asked.

'Sarah's a nurse, and I thought she might advise us on what to do.' I handed her a few sheets of paper. 'You need to read it.'

The heading on the first page was 'Symptoms of Bipolar Disorder.' Sabiha stood reading the handout as I waited next to her. When she finished a few minutes later, she gaped at me in wonder. 'This description fits Mum to a T. I've always known the name of her illness, but I've never really understood it.'

She swayed, her face dazed. I led her to sit on a bench next to the bike rack. 'Now I can see there were signs all along. She did all these things.' She read from the paper. *'Spending money recklessly, hyperactivity, high energy levels, inappropriate behaviour, mystical experiences.* It's just that we didn't know.'

I waited, letting her process.

'Why didn't she tell me?' Sabiha sounded betrayed. 'If I'd known, I could have watched over her.'

'She probably didn't know herself.' I sat next to her, our legs pressed together. 'Sarah told me that many people who come from overseas don't know how to translate the medical jargon. My sister included contact details for the CATT team.' I flipped the handout to the last page. 'You know the Crisis Assessment Treatment Team, that professionals or family members can call in an emergency.'

'I don't think I need to. Mum seems to be taking her medication again.'

'Okay...' I folded the handout and returned it to her. 'It's there if you need it.' As she took it, our hands touched.

'I can't believe you did this.' She held my hand.

'That's what friends do.' I gripped her hand gently. I wanted more, so much more, but I would not put myself out there anymore. She had to make the first move. She leaned in. It was going to happen. She was going to kiss me.

'Hey, lovebirds,' Brian called out as he approached.

Anger coursed through me. Damn Brian. He'd ruined my moment again. I watched him and Sabiha bicker as I calmed myself down.

Brian caught sight of of the paper in Sabha's hands and snatched it. 'What's this?'

She grabbed the pamphlet back. 'What do you care?'

'Of course I care,' Brian said. 'We're friends.'

'Yeah, right,' she muttered under her breath.

'Sabiha, what's going on?' Brian asked.

'If you were a *real* friend, you wouldn't have to ask that question,' she shot back.

'What does that mean?' Brian demanded. 'I *am* a real friend.'

'A *real* friend cares about what's going on in your life.' She gestured at Jesse. 'A *real* friend doesn't dump you as soon as something better comes along.'

Is that all we were? Friends. Was her kiss a pity kiss, one of gratitude? I dropped her hand.

'A *real* friend would understand that you have a life and can't be at their beck and call twenty-four-seven,' Brian said.

'A *real* friend would sense when you're in need.' She stood, and they were facing off.

'A *real* friend would tell you something was going on instead of taking pot-shots,' Brian shouted.

'Enough.' I stood between them. I had to calm this situation, or I would never understand if Sabiha really liked me.

'He's the one who—'

'She—' Brian and Sabiha spoke over each other.

'Cool it!' I shouted. 'Brian, we've been friends a long time.' I placed my hand on Brian's chest. 'You do sometimes get caught up in new things and forget about everyone else.'

Brian stared at the ground and kicked a pebble with his shoe.

I turned to face her. 'And Sabiha, you can't expect people to guess when something is wrong. You have to tell them.'

'I guess,' she said, chastened.

'Now, are you two making up?' I asked as I looked from one to the other.

Brian made a face.

She sucked in her lips to stop a smile.

'All right, Dad.' Brian grabbed me into a hug.

'Get off me!' I tried to push Brian's arms off. Watching us grapple, Sabiha burst into laughter and grabbed my arm. Brian threw his arm around her and pulled her in so that she was between me and Brian. Laughing, I pressed my chest against her back while Brian was up against her front. Maybe it was better to be friends. To slowly find our way to each other. I needed to stop being so impatient and just let it be. My hands relaxed around her and Brian, contentment filling me.

'Oooh, an orgy,' Dina said as she and Gemma came around the corner, Adnan following.

'We need one more girl for this orgy!' Brian grabbed Dina's arm and pulled her into the circle. We laughed at Dina's giggles as Brian tried to pash her. Our laughter was infectious, and Dina started up, too.

'Let her go!' Gemma beat her hands against Brian's back.

'There's room for you too.' Brian turned to Gemma.

'Yuck,' Gemma exclaimed as she stopped hitting him.

The bell rang, and we all moved away from each other, suddenly self-conscious, straightening our clothing as we headed to class. Sabiha glanced at me shyly as she straightened her clothes. There was definitely a spark. Definitely more than friends.

'What's going on with Sabiha?' Brian asked as we walked home from school.

'A lot. I'll let her tell you.'

Brian sucked on his lips and looked at me moodily.

'Call her, like you promised,' I urged.

'Okay.' Brian sighed.

'What's been going on with you? You've been distant lately.'

'Nothing.' Brian put his hand through his hair. 'Just busy.'

'You're spending a lot of time with Adnan, playing soccer.' I wanted to give him the opportunity to talk about Adnan.

He glanced at me sideways. 'Yeah. I like soccer.'

'Okay. Just don't ignore everyone else in your life for this new, exciting thing.'

Brian hitched his backpack higher, his jaw tight, not saying anything.

'You haven't come over for homework. Are you doing okay at school?'

'I'm fine,' he snapped.

He was lying, but I knew better than to push it. I had to let him talk to me first. And hopefully, he'd call Sabiha and repair that relationship. We split at my house.

Chapter 10

The rest of the week flew by. The gang hung around together at school, and all our conversations were about the party.

I wasn't as excited. I didn't do well at group events with too many people but was swept up in the excitement with everyone else. I kept glancing at Sabiha. Maybe this could be an opportunity for us?

I was trying on my costume in my bedroom when I thought I heard the front door open and close. I assumed I was imagining it when I didn't hear anyone speaking. I put on the dark pants that were my Zorro costume, wincing at how they moulded to my legs. Anger prickled my scalp. I put on the top. It, too, was skin-tight, the deep V sliding down my chest. 'Sarah,' I yelled. 'What the hell have you done?'

'Come out here so I can see!' Sarah shouted back.

I stalked out of my bedroom, fury making my legs stiff. 'Sarah, I hope this is your idea of a joke.' I lifted my head and saw Sabiha. She wore a trench coat, her shapely legs visible above blue knee-high boots. Her dark hair draped around her shoulders, red lipstick lighting up her face, making her green eyes brighter.

I blushed as I realised she was examining the open-necked V and my visible chest and arms. I'd bulked up since going to the gym, and the costume emphasised all the bulk. There was admiration on Sabiha's face, and I straightened. She saw I'd caught her gaze, and she blushed.

'Doesn't he look great, Sabiha?' Sarah approached and pinched my arms. 'Everyone can see his muscles.'

'Um, yeah, he does.' Sabiha sipped her drink, her cheeks flushed.

'I'm *not* going like this.' I pushed Sarah's hands away.

'Jesse...' a feeble voice called from the back of the house. 'Come here, please, so I can see you?'

Sarah laughed and pushed me towards the door. 'Go show Mum how hot you are.'

I narrowed my eyes at Sarah, and she shoed me away. 'Bring Mum out here so she can meet Sabiha,' she called out.

I broke my stride and looked at her. She knew I cared about Sabiha, and when she met my mum, she might judge her.

'It'll be fine,' she urged. Sarah nodded, telling me it was going to be okay. Introducing Mum to our friends and potential love interests was the true Litmus test of character. The way they reacted decided if they were keepers. I knew Sarah was right. It was time for Sabiha to meet Mum and for me to know whether she was a keeper. There was no point in being infatuated with someone who would not accept Mum as she was, but I was scared. The way Sabiha reacted to Mum decided whether I would ever again look at her the same way. If she rejected Mum or was unkind, then she was done. I would never look at her the same way. While my feelings might still be engaged, I wouldn't consider her. I had to protect my mum from harm.

Mum gasped when I entered her bedroom. 'You look so handsome. Just like Reggie.'

'Thank you Mum.' I self-consciously tilted my hat before I bent and kissed her. 'Did you want to come out and meet Sabiha?'

Mum gasped, putting her hand through her hair. 'She's here?'

I nodded.

'Yes, please.' Mum smiled, a dimple appearing on her cheek. 'I'm so excited.' She clasped her hands in front of her, her arms wobbling. I helped her from her bed into the wheelchair. 'Do I look alright?' She peered around me at the vanity.

'Hand me my hairbrush!' She gestured to her vanity.

I moved out of the way.

Mum brushed her hair, smoothing down the blonde tendrils.

'You look beautiful.' I kissed her on the cheek as I took the brush back.

'You're such a sweet boy.' She squeezed my hand. 'Let's go.' She took a deep breath.

I wheeled her down the hall on stiff legs, my stomach rolling, pleading in my head, 'please be kind.'

As Sarah introduced them Sabiha looked at me, her gaze softening.

'Jesse has told us so much about you.' Mum's voice was small. Her first instinct was always to make herself invisible. She reached out her hand to Sabiha, the dimpled rolls of fat on her arm shaking as she held it in the air.

'Nice to meet you too.' Sabha clasped her hand.

They made small talk for a few minutes, and I relaxed as I watched Sabiha talk to Mum normally. Some people reacted with embarrassment, struggling to look at Mum as if her obesity was contagious. You could see the judgement on their face as they scrutinised her size, a thought bubble above their head as they castigated her for letting herself become so big. Sabiha didn't do that. I felt myself falling even more under her spell.

Now that dilemma was solved, my thoughts turned back to my costume and leaving the house in such a tight outfit. 'I'm getting changed,' I said when there was a lull in the conversation.

'Into what?' Sarah was panicked. 'You haven't got another costume.'

'Peter Parker,' I said smugly.

'No!' Sarah howled. 'Tell him he looks great, Mum.'

'You look very handsome, Jesse,' Mum said. 'Do you think so?' She turned to Sabha.

Sabiha examined me from head to toe, warmth in her gaze. This was the look I'd seen sometimes when she and Brian flirted, a teasing glint as she telegraphed her approval.

'That's a great costume,' she pronounced.

'They got to you,' I said.

She shook her head and smiled.

I relaxed and looked at her approvingly, registering her cleavage peeking through the partially open trench coat. 'Okay, you win.' I lifted my hands in surrender.

Mum smiled at Sabiha gratefully. Sarah headed for the TV cabinet. 'Photo time.' She held a camera.

'Oh, no,' I groaned.

'Yes, yes!' Sarah shouted as she pulled Sabiha off the sofa and pushed her toward me. She watched us through the viewfinder. 'Take off the trench coat,' she commanded.

Sabiha took off her trench coat, and I finally saw her in her full body-hugging outfit. She was spectacular, her waist tiny, her bosoms spilling over the cups, her legs looking like they stretched forever. I gulped, struggling to breathe.

Sarah snapped a few photos. 'Okay, put your arm around her,' she instructed.

I gently curved my arm around Sabiha's waist. She felt so fragile and dainty under my hand.

'You do the same,' she said to Sabiha.

Tentatively, Sabiha hooked her fingers through my belt loop, feeling my back, sending shivers down my spine as I felt her brushing against my skin through the silk shirt.

'You look fabulous.' Sarah continued snapping.

We relaxed, and she sank against me. My hand firmed around her waist.

'Okay, look at each other,' Sarah said.

I looked into her green eyes. Thick eyelashes framed them, and her lips were moist. As we gazed at each other, she licked her lips. My gaze followed her tongue. She gasped. My hand tightened on her waist, and I brought her closer, fighting the urge to kiss her. Her gaze searched my face as if this was the first time she was seeing me.

I took a deep breath, my chest pushing into hers. I needed to break this tension. 'It's okay.' I nudged my head toward Sarah. 'I didn't charge the battery.'

Sarah smacked the camera. 'Damn, it's finished.'

'Told you.' I smiled and let go of her, clenching my hand from yanking her back against me where she belonged.

'We'd better get going,' she said.

'It's only six o'clock. Wait in Jesse's room until it's time for the party. That way, you can make a grand entrance with your costumes.' Sarah pushed us away from the front door and down the hall.

'But we should help Brian,' Sabiha protested.

Sarah cut her off. 'Greg and his mates have done plenty of party set-ups.' She closed my bedroom door behind us.

Sabiha stood in the middle of the room, a bewildered look on her face as she stared at her feet.

'Would you like to sit down?' I pushed my office chair toward her, and she sat down obediently.

She looked around my bedroom shyly. My room was always neat. That's what came from being the one who vacuumed and cleaned the house.

'Thanks,' I mumbled as I sat on the bed.

'What for?'

'For being nice to my mum.'

'Why didn't you tell me?' she asked.

I shrugged. 'She has hypothyroidism. Her thyroid doesn't produce enough hormones, and her metabolism is slow. It doesn't matter what she eats or what she tries to do, she's obese.'

'Has she always been in a wheelchair?'

'Just in the last couple of years. It's difficult for her to move otherwise.'

'I still wish you'd told me... It would have made a lot of stuff a lot easier...'

I shrugged again. I never knew how to tell people? Do I say my mum is morbidly obese, so please don't be mean to her? Sabiha looked at me in sympathy, and I relaxed under her gaze. She got it.

She turned and examined my room, her eyes lighting up as she examined the three tall bookshelves that took up a wall. 'How did you get hold of so many books?' She touched the spines with her fingertips as she looked at the titles.

I shivered, imagining her touching me.

'You have one glaring omission.' She gave me a stern look. 'You don't have any of Stephenie Meyer's books.'

I laughed. 'They're under the bed.'

'That'd be right.' She turned back to the shelves. 'I know you secretly love them even though you pretend you hate vampire stories.'

'Have you read this one?' I stood behind her, my arm reaching for a book over her head, my voice a whisper against her ear. I handed her *Wuthering Heights* by Emily Brontë, my hand floating around her shoulders so that I was almost embracing her.

She shook her head, and her hair brushed against my face. I wanted to be her Heathcliff and for her to be my Cathy. I heard Heathcliff in my head, *"If you ever looked at me once with what I know is in you, I would be your slave."*

'You'd like it. It's a gothic romance.' My breath fanned her hair.

Our eyes met. My cheek was right next to her mouth. I inclined my head, and my lips gently brushed hers, like the caress of a feather. I waited. Giving her the chance to back away. She leaned in and kissed me. My hands came to rest on her shoulders, and I pulled her to me, the book pressed between us like a chaperone as we kissed.

I lifted my head, wanting to tell her I was her slave, and under her spell forevermore. I rubbed her arms and leaned down, wanting to kiss her again, but she stiffened imperceptibly.

She looked uncomfortable, her body stiffening again. That was enough. I had to bide my time. I planted a soft kiss on her cheek and stepped away.

'You want to listen to music?' I moved to the computer on my desk.

She nodded and read the back cover of the book. 'Sounds like my sort of novel.'

It was described as a vindictive, passionate love story set amongst the wild Yorkshire moors.

'You can borrow it if you like,' I said. *Then when I tell you I'm your slave, you'll know my love is as passionate as Heathcliff's, although hopefully without the tragic ending.*

'Thanks.' She glanced at her watch. 'Perhaps we'd better forget the music; we should go.'

I nodded and held the bedroom door open.

Sarah kissed Sabiha's cheek as we entered the living room. 'Have a great night.'

'Come again,' Mum said.

I leaned down and kissed Mum before we left. 'She's a special one,' Mum whispered against my cheek. I squeezed her hands in agreement.

As we walked, our hands brushed against each other. My fingers gently tugged her. She didn't look at me as she clasped my hand. Music blared from Brian's house.

I stopped, and she turned to look at me. I needed to say something, and declare my feelings once and for all.

'Let's go, silly.' She tugged me toward Brian's house.

I sighed. It could wait. I had to be happy with the progress we'd made so far. She'd kissed me. She'd held my hand. I had to trust in her physical reaction.

Sabiha knocked on the front door, and Brian opened it. He was wearing a lycra green suit covered with black question marks. Sabiha dropped my hand and hugged Brian. 'You look amazing!' she yelled. 'Don't you think, Jesse?'

I smiled, pushing away the stab of jealousy that engulfed me as she stood in Brian's arms. I wanted to rip her away, push Brian and declare she's mine. 'Yeah, he sure does.' Heathcliff's possessive influence was already taking hold.

'I'll put this in my bag.' Sabiha held up *Wuthering Heights* and headed for Brian's parents' bedroom.

'I didn't think you had it in you.' Brian clapped me on the shoulder. 'I thought for sure you'd chicken out and come as Peter Parker.'

'I decided to be daring.' I licked my lips, wanting to tell Brian that Sabiha and I had kissed. Wanting him to know that we had crossed over to almost official, so he'd keep his hands off her.

'It's happening?' Brian exclaimed, waving his hand.

Now wasn't the time. I'd speak to him later.

'Yeah, I'm happy for you bro.' I slapped his back.

'Do you want a drink?' Brian walked down the corridor to the kitchen.

'I'll meet you there.' I walked out the back into the quiet backyard, taking a moment, fighting not to act like a jealous neanderthal about Sabiha and Brian's friendship. I knew nothing was going on there. They'd both told me as much. I needed to stop being insecure and reading into things.

I entered the kitchen to see Brian serving Sabiha Baileys, which she skolled from the bottle.

'Go Sabiha.' Brian exclaimed when she handed him back the bottle.

'Another please.' This time he half-filled a glass and, sipping her drink, she walked into the living room.

I got a can of Coke and followed her. Partygoers had arrived, some in costume, some in regular clothes.

Sabiha finished her drink. 'You want me to get you something?'

'I'm good.' I held up my Coke.

'You're such a geek.'

It sounded like she was making fun of me. Should I drink? Make her think I was cool. I hated the taste of alcohol, not to mention that I needed to be present to take care of Mum.

Sabiha returned to the kitchen table and got another drink. I debated about telling her to stop but thought better of it. There was a frenetic energy in her moves. A desperation that I was afraid to examine too closely. Gemma arrived in a Supergirl costume and asked Sabiha about Dina. Her boyfriend, Rob, was with her in a Superman costume. Sabiha curled her lip as she looked at them, and I could read the scorn on her face.

Brian was dancing to 'Push It' by Salt N' Pepper, and Sabiha approached him from behind and curved herself around him. I squeezed the can of Coke, crinkling the metal and making it froth at the top. He and Sabiha ground their hips against each other as they mouthed words.

They're friends. Nothing but friends, I chanted.

I followed Sabiha as she stumbled into the kitchen and slurped orange juice and vodka.

'How are you doing?' I asked.

'I'm having a blast,' she shouted, leaning against me.

With or Without You by U2 played, and she swayed as she sang. I took the glass from her hand and returned it to the table before lifting her arms and placing them on my shoulders. I sang in her ear as we slow-danced, wanting her to feel the weight of my words, understand what I felt for her. She leaned back in my arms and closed her eyes, hanging in mid-air. My heart beat faster as I looked at her beautiful face. I pulled her up, and she opened her eyes, her smile tender. She felt the same. I knew it. I put my hand under her chin, tugging her toward me, desperately wanting to kiss her. Suddenly, her face sobered, and she stiffened in my arms.

'Don't do that.' She pushed my hand away.

I tried to pull her back. 'I don't understand.'

'Just don't do it!' she shouted.

I watched her in puzzlement as she reached for the vodka. 'Just don't like me, okay.' She added orange juice and headed for the living room.

There was a tearing in my chest as hope leaked out. She didn't like me. I ran out to the backyard, hiding in the dark shadow under the awning, wiping tears from my face. I was such an idiot, thinking this would be my big moment. I took a deep, shuddering breath and put back my mask. The only saving grace was nobody would see my red-rimmed eyes. I was going home.

I heard shouting. 'Shit, Gemma's going to rip Sabiha's face off.' I heard someone shout as they slammed the fly screen open next to me. What happened to Sabiha? I was walking before I even knew it. I caught a cloud of satin on the dance floor as Gemma attempted to kick Sabiha, who was crawling on the floor, away from her. Rob carried Gemma away, and the two of them went into the corridor. I lost sight of Sabiha and pushed through the crowd. She was leaning against a wall. I followed her to the kitchen and found her pouring herself Jack Daniels.

'Sabiha, are you all right?' I held her arm and peered at her face in concern. There was a red mark on her cheek like someone had slapped her. I wanted to find Gemma and Rob and soundly kick them.

'I'm bloody marvellous,' Sabiha slurred, blinking sleepily at me.

I took the glass from her. 'You've had enough.'

'No, I haven't.' She hit my arm and reached for the glass.

'Everyone having a great time?' Brian shouted as he walked in.

'I am!' Sabiha shouted back and grabbed Brian. 'It's a great party.' She kissed him on the cheek.

'You want some?' Brian asked as he poured himself a drink. She reached for the glass. 'Fucking oath.'

'She's had enough.' I pushed between them.

Brian took a sip of the glass I had put down. 'It's a party.' Sabiha took the glass off him. 'I'll drink to that.'

'She can barely stand.' I grabbed the glass out of her hand.

'Don't be a bore,' Brian said. 'I'll keep an eye on her.'
Someone called his name, and he turned in the other direction.
Adnan broke through the crowd. He'd shunned a costume and
wore a white t-shirt and jeans. Brian hugged Adnan. 'I didn't
think you'd make it.'

'I came when the party started.' Adnan rubbed Sabiha's hair.
'Hey cuz. So are you a prostitute or Wonder Woman? I can't tell
the difference.'

'Ha, ha,' she sneered, brushing his hand away.

She swayed on her feet, her face turning white. I helped her
to a chair before she fell. She pushed me away. 'I'm fine.'

Brian and Adnan laughed and left the room. I knelt beside
her. 'Are you going to be sick?'

'No.' She shook her head, looking pale.

I got a glass of water and handed it to her.

'Thanks.' She handed back the empty glass. 'I feel better
now.'

I got a washcloth and ran it under the tap. I knelt back beside
her and held the damp washcloth against her forehead. 'You
need to ease up.'

'I'll be fine.' She took the washcloth from me. 'Brian will take
care of me.'

Blind rage filled me. I was right here, but it was all about
Brian. 'You need to understand one thing.' I squeezed her wrist.
'Brian takes care of himself first, last and always.'

'No, he doesn't.'

She tried to pry my hand away, but I didn't ease up.

'He's my best friend,' she said.

'He's been my best friend longer,' I told her. 'Brian will
always put fun first and responsibility second. Where is he
now?' I knew I was being unfair to Brian. His selfishness now
was uncharacteristic and a sign of other issues, but I wasn't in
the mood to be fair anymore. I wanted Sabiha to see me.

She didn't look like she was listening. Her eyes were closed, and she was listing to one side. Had she fainted? 'Did you hear me?' I shook her.

She pushed me away. 'Mind your business.'

'Fine.' I threw off her hand. 'You win.' I couldn't do this anymore. I couldn't keep begging her to see me, to think of me. She wanted Brian. Not me. I turned and left, making my way through the crowd. I adjusted my face mask so it collected my tears.

I opened my front door, attempting to be quiet. Sarah was sitting in the living room, watching a TV show. 'What are you doing home so early?' she asked, lowering the volume.

I didn't reply as I removed my boots and left them in the hallway. I walked into my bedroom and went to close the front door, but Sarah held it open. 'Jesse, what happened?'

'Not now.' I held the door, looking down at the ground.

'Did something happen with Sabiha?'

I looked away. She pushed into my room. 'What is it?'

'She likes Brian. It's always been Brian. I keep trying, but she just doesn't see me.'

'Brian?' Sarah asked. 'But I saw you two holding hands?'

'We were. We kissed. But then we went to the party, and Brian was there.' I let go of the door and whirled, the cloak swishing around me. I untied it from around my neck and flung it onto the bed. It draped slowly, increasing my frustration.

'And Brian likes Sabiha?' Sarah's tone held a questioning note.

'I don't know,' I lied. Brian hadn't come out to anyone but me, and I couldn't break his trust.

'But I thought Brian liked...'

I turned to Sarah, looking at her quizzically, as she didn't finish her sentence.

'What?'

'I thought Brian liked boys,' Sarah finally finished.

I put my hand through my hair, mussing it up as frustration coursed through me. I formed a fist and punched the wall, imagining I was punching Brian's face.

'Hey, hey.' Sarah approached and took my hand in hers. It was red and bleeding. 'Let's go to the kitchen.'

I followed her, shamefaced for being such a petulant child.

She got ice from the freezer and put it into a hand towel. 'Was Sabiha alright? I mean, had she been drinking?' Sarah asked as she slammed the freezer.

'Well yes, but—'

'That's it.' Sarah cut me off. 'She was just drunk and flirty. It means nothing.'

'It's more than that. She told me not to like her.'

Sarah frowned as she got the first aid kit and dabbed alcohol onto my cuts. 'What brought that on?'

'We were dancing.'

'What song?'

'U2. *With or without you.*'

'Oh.' Sarah made a sound like she understood something.

'What?' Jesse demanded.

'That's a full-on song. That's an "I love you" love song.'

I said nothing.

'You didn't tell her you loved her, did you?' She squeezed my hand, and I winced and moved it away.

'No.' I said, not meeting her gaze.

'Did you or didn't you?' she demanded.

'I didn't.'

Sarah started at me until I squirmed.

'I was about to.'

'There you go. You put too much pressure on her. She just realised she likes you and you're already at the "I love you stage." You freaked her out.'

'So. That doesn't mean she should have flirted with Brian.' I stood.

'It's Brian. She probably doesn't even think of him as a real guy, or a real flirtation. He's just a friend.' She patted my shoulder. 'Just wait and see. Tomorrow it will all be alright.'

I didn't want to believe her but hope again stirred in my heart. Sarah was always right. Maybe she was right about this too, and Sabiha just needed time to adjust. But then I remembered her face. Her discomfort and disquiet filled me again. Sarah was wrong. Sabiha didn't like me. I spent the night tossing and turning, not catching a wink of sleep.

Chapter 11

I finally fell into a restless sleep early in the morning. I heard the front door opening and then footsteps in the hall. My bedroom door burst open. I opened my eyes blearily to find Brian pacing up and down in front of my bed.

'What's wrong?' I sat up.

'I did something bad.' Brian put his thumb into his mouth and bit his fingernail. Oh, god. I felt nauseous. He and Sabiha hooked up. They were together. I didn't know how I was going to hear this.

'Sabiha found I was gay.' Brian winced.

'How did she find out?' I asked, pulling on a top and my jeans.

'She saw me with Adnan.' Brian glanced up, checking to see if it freaked me out.

'I'm not surprised?' I pulled on my t-shirt.

'Shit, he's firmly in the closet. Do you think anyone else knows?' Brian looked terrified.

'No, I only suspected because I know you.'

Brian sat despondently on my bed. 'I love him. I think he loves me.'

The way he said it broke my heart. With such hope and trepidation. Is that what I sounded like with Sabiha?

'And if he finds out Sabiha kissed me, he won't take it well.' He bit his fingernail again. 'I don't understand why she did it after seeing me with him.'

I spun away, hiding my face. Sabiha kissed Brian? She did it after kissing me? After knowing that Brian was gay? Did she love him so much that she wanted to turn him? I realised I wasn't listening to Brian and smoothed out my face, and turned back.

'Do you want breakfast?' I asked, needing to buy myself some time to process.

'Yes, please.' Brian followed me to the kitchen. He kept talking about Beckham, the code-name he'd given Adnan in public, as I made pancakes for all of us. Why had Sabiha kissed Brian? Was it to get back at Adnan, who was always a thorn in her side, or was she just so desperately in love with Brian that she had to try everything? As I poured batter into the pan and made pancakes, I realised I had to know why she did it?

Brian hung out for breakfast and then went home, saying he was going to sleep the whole day. I fought the urge to call Sabiha. This was a conversation I had to have face-to-face.

Monday, I waited impatiently for Brian to show up at the front of my house, but when he didn't arrive, I walked to his and knocked on the door. Greg answered and let me in. I knocked on Brian's door and entered. His room was dark, and he was still in bed.

He sat up, his hair mussed, wearing a singlet. 'What time is it?'

'Time for school.' I opened the curtains.

Brian flinched and covered his face with his arm. 'I don't feel well.'

'No, you're not doing this to me.' I threw his jeans on the bed. 'You are not leaving me to clean up your mess.'

'I'm sick, I'm telling you.'

'Yes, sick with guilt. You need to go to school and talk to Sabiha. Deal with the mess you made.'

'Seriously, I'm sick.'

I peered closer. He looked pale, but it wasn't anything his excessive drinking at the party couldn't explain.

'You're coming to school.' I could not face the thought of seeing Sabiha by myself. How could I talk to her without exploding? I yanked Brian up. He blanched and ran down the hallway and into the bathroom, slamming the door behind him. I walked down and heard retching. Damit, he really was sick.

'Okay. You stay home. I'll bring your homework,' I said through the door and ambled slowly to school, feeling nauseous. My first two sessions were psychology with Sabiha. I arrived when the bell had already gone, and the corridors were empty by the time I'd reached the classroom. I walked in as the teacher was about to commence, sitting at the back.

Sabiha glanced at me and quickly away, covering her face with her hair as she avoided looking at me. The teacher gave us instructions to work with our partners. I walked to her and dropped the folder on her desk. She flinched.

'I've followed up on those articles in the library,' I announced as I sat down and read through my notes in a monotone voice. When I'd prepared the research last week, I had imagined this moment, the two of us sitting pressed up against each other as we pored over the notes; instead I wanted to be anywhere but here. 'Is there anything you have to add?'

'Um, no...' Her voice was barely above a whisper.

I grabbed his folder and went to stand, but changed my mind. I had to know. Whatever it cost me, however hard it was to hear the truth, I had to know. I dropped the folder on the desk again and turned in the chair to face her. 'I want to know why you did it?' I demanded.

She couldn't meet my eyes. 'It just happened—'

'Cut the crap,' I interrupted. 'Why Brian, of all people?'

'What do you mean?' She looked up. 'You know I've always liked Brian.'

'Yes, but he's had the talk with you,' I said. 'So I don't understand why—'

'Yes, we had the talk.' She was getting angry. 'He was the one who kissed me. He was the one who changed his mind about us being more than friends.'

'He kissed you?' I asked.

'Yes,' she said.

I stared out the window behind her, seeing the perplexed look on my face in my reflection. Brian said that she saw him with a boy. That she knew he was gay and that she'd kissed him afterwards, trying to turn him. Or had I misunderstood that?

'Jesse, I'm sorry about what happened between us,' she said. 'I shouldn't have led you on when I always had feelings for Brian.'

She really didn't know that Brian was gay? Did Brian assume that she saw him when she walked in on him and his secret beau, but she actually saw nothing? She didn't actually know anything about him?

'Have you talked to Brian since Saturday?' I asked.

'We haven't had a chance—'

'This is a mess.' I put my hands through my hair. Shit, I didn't have any choice. I had to tell her the truth. Bloody Brian, always leaving me to sort out his mess. 'Sabiha, you must know that Brian is—'

'Class, please face the front,' the teacher said.

I sighed in frustration and returned to my desk, tapping my fingers on the tabletop as I moodily stared ahead. Brian had to sort this out. I avoided Sabiha for the rest of the day, which was easy. She seemed just as determined to avoid me.

After school, I went home to take care of Mum and then left the house to go to Brian's. As I approached, I saw Sabiha run out, tears on her face, her hand covering her mouth as she sobbed.

I felt a burst of relief. Brian had told her. I took her arm and walked her down the street. 'So Brian told you he was gay?'

'When did he tell you?' How come I was the last one to find out?' Anger and shock warred her face.

'I always knew he was gay.'

'Well, I didn't,' Sabiha said flatly.

'Will you be okay?' I asked.

She nodded, looking embarrassed. 'I'd better get going.' She edged down the road.

'Okay.' I watched her go. It was done. We were done. I'd hoped for so long, but now it was time to let it go. She chose Brian, and even though Brian didn't choose her back, it didn't matter. She'd made her choice, and now I had to move on.

I walked back to Brian's house to see how he was doing. The front door opened as I walked up, and Adnan exited.

'See you.' Adnan hopped down to the curb.

I watched him walk to his car parked a few houses away, anger and pity warring inside me. Poor Sabiha. I'd been struggling being in a love triangle with my best friend, yet Sabiha was in a love triangle with her cousin. I shook my head, pushing the thought out of my head. Not my problem anymore.

Greg opened the door for me. I knocked on Brian's bedroom and entered. He was sitting on his bed, his back against the wall, a pillow on his raise knees, his face in the pillow.

'Brian,' I called his name.

He lifted his face, and I saw his tear-streaked face. 'He left me,' Brian gasped. 'Adnan left me. He said he doesn't love me, and he left me.'

I sat on the bed and hugged him tight, holding him as he sobbed.

Greg opened the door and walked in. 'What's going on?'

'He had a breakup,' I said, unsure how much he knew about Brian.

'Oh, I thought he and Sabiha were so cute together.' Greg backed away and closed the door behind him.

There was my answer. He knew nothing about Brian.

'I thought Sabiha knew about us on Saturday. That she saw me with Adnan, but she was so shocked when she walked in on us today.'

What a disaster! My heart broke for her. I wanted to comfort her. *Stop it, Jesse. She made her preferences known.*

'Is Adnan out?'

Brian shook his head. 'That's why he dumped me. He's too scared his family will find out. That Sabiha will out him, and then his parents will lose it. He wants me to make sure she doesn't talk.'

'Sabiha won't do that.' I rubbed his arm. 'She'll protect him for their sake.'

'How am I going to get over him?' Brian asked. 'I love him. We're meant to be together.'

I listened to him talk, feeling like a hypocrite. I thought Sabiha and I were together, yet here we were now, broken-hearted.

I trudged to school, Brian beside me. We looked like two sad sacks. Brian's face was pale, with dark circles under his eyes, probably from crying all night. My face was paler than usual, my eyes red. It was obvious I had been crying, too. I was dreading school and being around Sabiha. I wanted to avoid her as much as possible but knew I couldn't abandon Brian. He wanted to stay home, but his father forced him to come to school.

Dina was waiting for us at the front. 'So you heard what happened to Sabiha?' she said when she saw us.

Brian and I shared a look. 'No, what happened?'

'I thought you knew. The two of you look so sad.'

I didn't speak.

'Sabiha's mother had a breakdown at the shopping centre yesterday. The police took her to the hospital. When they went to the house, they said that Sabiha didn't have anyone able to care for her and the Department of Human Services had taken her into care.'

'No, no.' Brian cried, covering his hand with his mouth. 'They took her away.'

My knees felt weak, and I had to sit on the bench. I saw her face again, her fear when she talked about her mother being sick.

She'd been afraid of being taken away, about losing her home. I thought she was exaggerating, that it would never happen. After all, she had family, but it did.

'How did this happen?' I asked. 'She has a grandfather, an aunt.'

'Her grandfather can't take care of her. He needs someone to care for him. And Sabiha won't live with her aunt.'

Brian and I shared a glance.

'Oh,' I said. Sabiha probably couldn't stand the thought of being under the same roof as Adnan after learning his secret. How awkward.

'Do you know why?' Dina asked Brian.

He looked away; guilt telegraphed on his face.

Just then, Adnan stopped at the school fence and got out of his car. Brian trotted to the fence. 'Adnan, hi.' Adnan snubbed him, walking past him and into the school.

'What happened with you and Adnan?' Dina demanded.

Brian shook his heed, wiping away a tear. 'He's not interested in being my friend anymore.'

Dina mulled that over, not satisfied. 'Is it because you came out to him?'

Brian gasped, and I looked at her in surprise.

'How do you know?' Brian asked.

'I have eyes, don't I? Still, it's not like homosexuality is catching. I didn't think Adnan was so shallow.' Her eyes narrowed with suspicion.

'What's going to happen to Sabiha?' I asked, changing the subject before she connected the dots.

'I don't know.' Dina's shoulders slumped. 'She's been taken into care while they determine a safe environment for her. I've been texting her to check on her.' She held up her phone.

'Has she replied?'

Dina showed me her phone. There was a one-word response, 'tired.'

I met her gaze. She looked as worried as I was.

I took my mobile out and took a deep breath. I needed to reach out to her, push aside my wounded pride, and let her know I was there for her. 'Just checking in. Going to miss you at school.'

Brian took out his phone and typed, 'Miss you, bitch.'

I rolled my eyes. 'You're such a prick.'

'What? If I wrote anything else, she'd know I was thinking of her with pity. That's the last thing Sabiha would want.'

'You're right,' I said.

We walked to class together, Dina sticking by us. 'Where's Gemma?' I asked.

'That racist isn't coming to school anymore. She's moved in with her boyfriend, Rob.'

I frowned. What had I missed?

We spent recess and lunch together, all of us subdued and bruised from our individual dramas. Dina told me about Gemma and their fight. She seemed broken. I couldn't help but wonder if more was going on, but I would not pry. Dina had always been a mystery, cloaking herself in drama. I couldn't help but feel there was something she hid below the surface.

Brian wanted to go to the oval at lunchtime.

'No, we're not doing that,' Dina said determinedly.

'Why? I want to play soccer.' Brian sounded like a petulant child.

'I knew it.' Dina sighed and put her hands on her hips. 'You want to get Adnan's attention, but it won't work. He has to hide who he is, and now with Bahra being in the hospital. That family is a powder keg, and Adnan is on edge. We are staying away.'

Brian and I gaped at each other. I hadn't thought Dina was so perceptive. Brian's shoulders relaxed. Dina didn't seem perturbed by the fact that he was gay, and I was relieved we had no more secrets.

'I've got a spot.' I led them to the elm tree. As we sat under the tree, I remembered the last time I was here with Sabiha, the hope and the way she'd looked at me. She'd definitely felt something, but it wasn't enough.

Brian and I walked home after school. When I opened my computer at home, Charlie's latest images about the zombie love story were there. The zombie girl was crushing on a human, but she kept feeling a strange hunger for him that she didn't recognise.

I stared at the images for a few minutes. Charlie had perfectly captured Sabiha's expression when she was contemplative in the zombie girl. I wondered what she was doing. None of us had heard any responses to our text messages. She'd only sent that one message to Dina.

I wanted to give up the comic book. What did it matter? There was no love story, just unrequited love, but it wouldn't leave my mind. It was almost like the graphic novel was giving me the opportunity to re-write my story with Sabiha. To make a new ending for us. In my dreams, I kept seeing the scene play out, the zombie girl speaking and Jasper, my doppelgänger, replied.

I woke up in the early hours of the morning and wrote captions for the scenes, sending them off to Charlie. I had to keep my commitment to Charlie, I told myself. He deserved better than having a friend drop out after he'd invested so much work. But it was more than that. I needed to work on the book. I needed something to hold on to of Sabiha. If I couldn't have her, at least my fictional alter-ego could.

The next two weeks passed in a fog, and then Dina told me Sabiha was returning. The department had brought her home, and her aunt would stay with her.

I watched from the library window as Dina stooped at a car. She opened the door and tugged Sabiha out, leading her to the school. Sabiha was a girl transformed. Gone was the girl with confidence and verve. This Sabiha looked broken and worn out. Her shoulders were stooped, and she looked at the school as if it was a haunted house. To her, it probably was. There were only questions and problems waiting.

Brian stood next to me. 'She looks so sad.'

'Yes, she does.' I straightened my shoulders, making my voice strong. I couldn't waver. Sabiha was a friend only. Anything we had was done. I had to put her in the past and look to the future.

'I'll go talk to her first, and then you come after I've smoothed the path.' I tugged at my shirt collar nervously.

'Thank you.' Brian squeezed my hand.

I walked to the front of the school, feeling like a gladiator heading to battle. I couldn't show any weakness. I was here as a friend, nothing more.

Dina walked past me, her eyes red and face wet. Why was she crying? I didn't pry. She wanted her privacy.

I walked to the front of the table. 'How are you?'

'Okay,' she whispered, her eyes on the ground.

'I collected your English homework.' I handed her an envelope.

She took out the sheets and checked them. I'd collected from all her classes, talking to all her teachers, even the ones we didn't share.

'Why did you do this?' She crushed the envelope in my fist. 'After what I did to you.'

'You did nothing to me.'

'What do you mean? I led you on.'

'No.' I fought to hold my gaze steady. I couldn't waver. 'I let you.'

We could only salvage our friendship if I took responsibility for what had happened. I'd kept trying to get her to like me, even when I knew she was interested in Brian. I should have read the signs and let things be as they were.

'I always knew you didn't like me the way I liked you.' I sighed and put my hands on the tabletop. 'I thought that if enough time passed...'

I looked away, trying to get myself under control. When I looked back, it was as if her hand was inching towards mine. 'But that's not important anymore.' I took a step backwards, and her hand landed in the space where mine had been. I couldn't stand for her to touch me with pity. I had to maintain my distance.

I saw Brian peering at us from the corner of the school building.

'Do you want to talk to him?' I asked.

She followed my gaze. When Brian saw we were watching, he ducked back. Sabiha hesitated.

'He wants to apologise for what he did.' I kept my gaze steady on where Brian had been. I didn't trust myself to look at her.

'Okay,' she said.

I signalled for Brian to come over. 'I'll leave you guys to talk.'

I walked toward my locker, meeting Dina on the way. 'She's talking to Brian,' I said. 'Let's leave them to it.'

Dina turned around and stepped in with me. 'Are you okay?' I asked as we walked upstairs to our lockers.

'Yeah.' She sighed. 'A broken heart is a heavy burden.'

I stiffened, thinking she was talking about me, but then I looked at her face. She was talking about herself.

'Do you want to talk about it?' I asked.

She shook her head, tears starting.

***

We huddled around Sabiha during our classes. I'd thought it would be awkward in our solo classes together, but she was like a bird with a broken wing, listless. She sat in class and took notes but would quickly zone out, a sad look in her eyes.

'How is your mum?' I asked as we walked out of class.

She shrugged. 'I don't know. I haven't seen her.'

I stopped her, taking hold of her arm. 'Why? What happened?'

Sabiha looked at me and quickly away. 'She said something—' Her voice broke, and she couldn't finish the sentence. 'She said she cursed the day she fell pregnant with me.'

My eyes widened, and I had to fight my instinct to hug her, feel her body against mine and comfort her, but I couldn't. 'She didn't mean it. You have to know she didn't believe it.' I held her gaze, trying to instill my belief in her.

'But she did.'

A tear drifted down her cheek. It took every ounce of my strength to stop myself from wiping it. I handed her a handkerchief instead.

'She wanted to marry a Serb man, but my aunt and grandfather chased him away. Mum only married my father to get away from them. She didn't want me.'

'I don't believe that. And you don't either. She was sick when she said that.'

'How do I know?' She asked softly.

'You just have to trust your heart,' I told her, feeling like a hypocrite as I lied to my treacherous heart.

At lunchtime, we sat at the front of the school. Adnan passed by with his new girlfriend. Brian sat up straight, straining forward as he waited for Adnan to look our way. Adnan ignored us. Brian slumped. Dina took his hand.

'At least I have you,' Brian said, looking around at us. 'My Sassy Saints.'

'Say what?' I asked.

'We're from St Albans, and we're sassy. Sassy Saints.'

'It's perfect,' Dina said, hugging Brian and Sabiha while I leaned against Brian.

I looked at Sabiha. Maybe we weren't meant to be together, but we were best friends. That was enough.

Chapter 12

'Are you sure you're up for this?' I asked Charlie as we stood in the doorway of the foyer and peered into the large room where publishers were seated. We were attending the Writers Victoria speed dating session.

I turned to Charlie when he didn't answer. He was wearing his noise-cancelling headphones and shaded glasses to block out the bright lights. His usual garb was loose cotton tracksuit pants and a black cotton t-shirt, with his Nike runners. We'd caught the early train to avoid the crowds and spent the morning at the State Library until the speed dating session started. I'd wanted to dress up more professionally but couldn't be too out of step with Charlie, who was very particular about fabrics he could wear. I'd bought new jeans, forgone my usual loose pair, and got a fitted pair, with a collared short-sleeved plaid shirt. I looked casual dressy.

I smiled brightly. 'You good?' I lifted my thumb in the universal sign of okay.

Charlie nodded, his face blank. Other people were waiting in the foyer, and they jostled Charlie, who flinched. I saw a quiet corner near the back and pointed. Charlie nodded and followed. I held up my hand, showing for him to wait for me.

I approached the front desk and the dark-haired woman standing behind it. 'I'm Jesse James, and that is Charlie Lacertosa.' I pointed to Charlie, who was watching us.

'Of course. I'm Elizabeth, and I'll be helping you out today. Just follow me.' She stepped out from behind the counter, and I waved to Charlie.

He weaved through the crowd but hit a group of women talking and stopped dead. I pushed through and approached him.

'Excuse me,' I said to the women, urging them out of the way. They moved, and Charlie followed me.

We approached Elizabeth. 'We've set up a green room for the two of you.' She led us to the back.

'Excuse me,' a woman stepped in front of Elizabeth. 'Why do they get to cut in line? We've been here much earlier.'

'They're not cutting the line. These two writers are part of a different program,' Elizabeth diplomatically evaded, protecting Charlie's privacy.

Before I'd signed us up for the speed dating, I'd contacted the Quill & Quire Collective and explained that Charlie was on the spectrum and couldn't take part in an echoey room with all the writers and publishers together. The organisation had arranged a separate room for Charlie and a few other disabled writers. We walked through a corridor with glass partitions at the front, passing by a woman in a wheelchair and two men sitting together, their hands elegantly signing to each other.

We entered a small room at the back with only a table and chairs. It was some sort of small meeting room with only a window overlooking the lane. Charlie wouldn't have been comfortable with the partitioned office where he could observe people passing. Charlie sat in the corner, taking off his noise-cancelling headphones and glasses.

'The toilets are to your left and the kitchen to your right.' Elizabeth gestured. 'Do you need anything else?'

I glanced at Charlie, who shook his head.

'We have Peter Clarke from Gordonio coming at 9.30 am, and Catherine Duong from Welston at 10.30 am.'

'Thank you.'

Elizabeth smiled and left.

Charlie took out his book and read. I took out our sample pages and laid them out on the table. I took out my cue cards and began rehearsing my pitch, my voice getting loud.

Charlie glanced at me with annoyance, and I whispered once again. I looked at my watch. Twenty minutes. Nerves hit me.

'I'm just going to the loo,' I lied to Charlie and stepped out, nervously pacing up and down the corridor. People assumed that because Charlie didn't show expression, he didn't feel emotion. But I knew he did. Even though he was dealing with the day well so far, I knew it had cost him. He was holding his book with a white-knuckle grip as he read, a sure sign that he was struggling.

It had taken a lot of planning to get here. I'd set up an itinerary and showed Charlie the route via Google Maps to prepare him for the journey. Now that we were in the room and just needed the editors to come to us to pitch, it was the culmination of everything.

Our whole big pitch. I'd told Charlie that this was just a fun opportunity, that it wasn't about getting published, but I'd lied. I desperately wanted to be published. I wanted this book to have an audience. The book had originally started as my big romantic gesture for Sabiha, but now that I had accepted that we were meant to be friends, I wanted this book to find a publisher for me and my family. My mother felt like she was burdening me and my sister with her care. If my novel was published, she would know that I wasn't being held back at all. Because of her, I had grit and resilience that I could channel into my life.

My phone beeped, and I opened the chat titled Sassy Saints.

'How's the city?' Brian typed.

I felt a pang of guilt for lying to my best friend, but I didn't want everyone to know that I was trying to get published. Then they'd keep asking what happened, and I'd feel like a failure if I didn't get a request.

'So jelly you're at a workshop while we're bored at school.'
Sabiha added.

Dina added an emoji of a smiley face with the tongue hanging
out.

I smiled. Brian's moniker of us being Sassy Saints had stuck.
Over the past month, we had drawn together as a friendship
group. My heart still felt a pang every time I saw Sabiha's name
pop up on my phone, but I was learning to value our friendship
and lay my achy heart to rest.

I took a photo from the window of the city before me, the
tall buildings and the tram electricity lines. 'My view.' After a
few moments, reaction emojis to my message appeared: a love
heart from Sabiha, thumbs up from Brian, and a smiley face
from Dina.

I returned to the office.

'Are you okay?' Charlie peered at me over his book.

'Sure, sure, yeah. I'm great.' I wiped my sweaty palms on
my jeans. I got my cue cards, wanting to re-read my pitch, and
dropped them, where they fluttered to the floor. 'Oh, shit.'
I bent and collected them. They were all out of order. Shit,
why hadn't I numbered them? The door opened, and a man
in ripped jeans and a loose-fitting shirt walked in, blonde hair
swept up in a bun and a neatly trimmed beard.

Charlie stood and walked around me. 'You're Peter Clarke
from Gordonio.'

Peter nodded confirmation.

'Good to meet you. I'm Charlie Lacertosa, and that is Jesse
James.'

I stood, the cue cards crumpled in my hands. Peter had
been clued in about Charlie and didn't offer his hand for a
handshake, so we just nodded at each other.

'Please, take a seat.' Charlie indicated the chair across the
table.

Peter sat, and Charlie sat across from him. I slid into my chair,
my cheeks flushed as I was completely flustered. I'd rehearsed my

pitch, but it had always been with my cue cards in my hand, the physical sensation of the cardboard cutting in my palm giving me confidence and comfort. All I had to do was look down and get my pitch and flow back into my head. Now I was completely panicked and couldn't remember a single thing.

'We're here to talk to you about our graphic novel, *Flesh and Love*,' Charlie said, back straight and voice firm. 'Saphire is a resilient girl who thrives in the post-apocalyptic world. Jasper is a vegetarian zombie who does not. Together, they undertake a cross-country trip to reunite Saphire with her mother. Saphire sees Jasper as necessary cargo to keep the other zombies at bay. Jasper thinks Saphire is the love of his life. Only one of them is right.'

Charlie flicked to the pages of the graphic and showed Peter the storyboard. 'In the first scene, Saphire is entering a shopping centre looking for supplies and zombies attack, but she kicks their arse. She finds Jasper chewing on the frozen vegetables in the frozen food section. He's a vegetarian and refuses to eat brains like the other zombies. She takes him prisoner, planning to use him to keep the others at bay.'

Charlie spoke calmly, tracing his drawings with his finger.

'How is it a love story? She's human, and he's a zombie?' Peter asked.

'That's the twist. She's actually a zombie too, but she can't accept it. Because to accept that would be to accept the truth that her mother is dead.'

'This is very impressive. What medium are you using?' Peter asked.

'Charcoal is my preferred medium, and then I scan the photos using my printer, a Canon Canon Scan LiDE220.'

Peter's eyebrow raised when he heard the model.

While I knew Charlie was articulate when he wanted to be, it still took me by surprise how he could take charge.

'You're our preferred publisher as you've published the Mikado Chronicles. Jesse and I are huge fans, and this is the inspiration for our graphic novel.'

'Have you completed the book?' Peter asked.

'Yes,' Charlie nodded. 'We have the written draft and art completed and ready to submit.'

Peter rubbed his beard. 'And if we publish, how will you be able to take part in publicity?'

'Jesse will undertake the face-to-face interview, and I'll do my portion via email. I have also started a YouTube channel where I post stills of my drawing process.' Charlie flicked on his phone and tapped the YouTube icon, holding it up for Peter. 'As you can see, I have 2000 subscribers, and each video gets an average of 3000 views.'

'That's impressive.' Peter handed Charlie back his phone. 'And you Jesse?'

'I have had short stories published in the *Star Weekly* and *Voiceworks*.' I flipped open my display folder, where I'd inserted copies of my published stories.

Peter glanced down, reading a paragraph from each page. 'You're both certainly talented. I'd love to look at your completed manuscript.' He handed his business card. 'Please submit it to me.'

I looked at Charlie and smiled. His face was blank, but there was a twinkle in his eye. He was excited too.

Peter stood, and we said our goodbyes.

'We did it.' I jumped on the spot, my excitement making me want to vibrate.

Charlie nodded. 'We did it.'

'Well, actually, you did. You were amazing.'

Charlie nodded, retreating to a corner. He put his headphones back on and his glasses, leaning his forehead against the cool wall.

I knew to leave him alone. This was the thing about social interactions, Charlie could do it through sheer force of will and engage in talking to people, but it left him depleted and exhausted. If he pushed too hard, he had a meltdown. In primary school, the teachers would ignore signs of his depletion and kept engaging him until he lost it and lay on the ground screaming. The classroom would get evacuated until his mother arrived at school and would calm him down. He'd usually not be at school for a few days after that.

In high school, he'd gotten better at coping, and the school was better at supporting him. He had a card that he could use to go to the Wellbeing office and have a timeout if he was getting in the danger zone. His parents had picked him up from school a few times, but he'd avoided those spectacular meltdowns.

I left the room and dashed up and down the corridor, working out my frenzied energy. I returned at 10.15 am to wait for our next publisher. At 10.25 am, Charlie took off his headphones and stood by the window, looking out.

'You okay?' I asked. 'I can do this solo if you need to take time out.'

He nodded. 'I can do it.'

The door opened at 10.31 and an Asian woman walked in, wearing a red silk shirt and black skirt, her long black hair glistening around her shoulders.

'I'm Catherine Duong.' She offered her hand, and I shook it. She extended it to Charlie, who looked at her blankly.

'Charlie doesn't shake hands,' I said.

'Of course.' She blushed and put her hand to her side.

We sat at the table and did our pitch, this time taking turns as we'd planned, the cue cards back in my palm and giving me the confidence to contribute.

Catherine requested a full pitch, too.

'Was she into it?' Charlie asked.

'Nah, she just asked to be polite.' Charlie didn't pick up tone and body language and required a translator.

'And Peter?' Charlie asked.

'He was definitely into it. I have a good feeling.' I felt a warm glow of satisfaction. This was the dream to have a publisher actually request your work.

'Route,' Charlie said.

I took out the map and went over the route we would take to return to the train station. I checked the schedule. 'We'll leave in 10 minutes.' I needed to minimise Charlie's interaction with the outside world. We would arrive at the train station with a few minutes to spare.

Charlie put on his headphones, and sunglasses and we left the building.

When we got to the train, Charlie got out his sketchbook and drew. I opened my backpack and took out the sandwiches his mum had packed for us, handing him his butter sandwich on white bread, the crusts cut off. He ate one-handed and continued drawing, his headphones blocking out the noise from the train carriage.

I took out my book and attempted to read, but my concentration was low. I imagined Sabiha's face when I got a request. Would she be proud of me?

We reached St Albans train station and walked home together.

'Listen, I don't want anyone to know we got a request.' Charlie had lifted his headphone to hear me.

'Why?' Disappointment pinged me. I'd been imagining my hero moment when I told the Sassy Saints that I'd actually gone to a speed dating session and received a request.

'We don't know if the publisher will take it or not. And I don't want my parents getting wind of it. They're going to start having more expectations of me to achieve my potential.'

I glanced at him. Even though his words sounded sarcastic, his voice was monotone. While his parents were very supporting of his needs, they still wanted to believe that Charlie could function and achieve like any other kid. His high grades in school just confirmed their belief. Charlie was gifted in Maths but struggled with English and other subjects. Anything with abstract concepts was opaque. He still achieved well in those subjects as he was on an individual needs plan, so teachers catered to his abilities, but his parents glossed over that when they bragged about his academic achievements. They would use this news to brag, and if their submission didn't eventuate in publication, they would just naively expect that he would get published and put more pressure on him to commercialise his art.

'Okay, we'll keep it to ourselves,' I agreed. Maybe it was better not to let anyone know. If I did, they'd want to read the book. Sabiha and I had just gotten to a good place. If she read the graphic novel and recognised herself in Saphire and me in Jasper, she might think I was still into her, and things would get awkward again.

Chapter 13

As we walked up, Dina and Sabiha were waiting for us at the school. 'Did you hear Sabiha's news?' Dina demanded as Brian and I approached.

Sabiha stared broodily into the distance. Looked like the news wasn't good.

'Her father called her. He didn't know that Sabiha was his daughter,' Dina's voice squeaked slightly. 'Her Mum told him that Sabiha was fathered by her ex-boyfriend Darko.'

'Okay, slow down, squeaky.' Brian urged Dina. 'Start at the beginning.'

Dina did, while Sabiha looked past us. When her mother, Bahra was pregnant with Sabiha, she told Sabiha's father that the baby was her ex-boyfriend's. He believed her and left. A few months ago, when family friends were visiting Sabiha, they realised she was the spitting image of her father Enes and went to see him, telling him about her. Sabiha found everything out when he called her house last night and spoke to her mother and then her grandfather.

Dina and Brian paired up, getting into the salacious details of Sabiha's parentage.

I approached Sabiha and sat next to her on the bench. 'How are you feeling?'

'Shit,' she spat, her voice wavering with fury. 'He wanted to talk to me last night. He's acted like I don't exist my whole life, and now I'm supposed to say hello daddy.'

'But he says he didn't know.' I remembered all the daydreams I'd had as a child that my dad wasn't really dead, instead, he was kidnapped, and then he escaped from his abductors and came home to us. It took me so many years to accept that he was truly dead. I couldn't understand how this wasn't a dream come true for Sabiha. She finally had a chance to have her father in her life.

'Bullshit. He's a doctor, but he believed a woman who was suffering from a Bipolar episode. He wanted to believe it because he was having an affair with his receptionist and wanted out. The only reason he's acting like he gives a fuck is because people in the community now know.' She crossed her arms over her chest, her gaze narrowed with anger.

I hesitated, not sure whether I should wade in. 'That's harsh,' I began gently.

'I don't give a shit. I spent sixteen years without a father. I do not need one now.' Her glistening eyes and fisted hands said something else. She wasn't as indifferent as she pretended.

'He's reaching out now. Shouldn't that count for something?' I gently lay my arm around her shoulder. It was the first time I'd attempted physical affection since the comic book party. I'd been too nervous to try to bridge the physical distance, but if anything called for affection, it was finding out you had a long-lost father who now wanted to find you.

'Puh-lease. Watch how quickly he disappears into the woodwork. This is just his five-minute attempt at redemption.' She was hunched, as if she was protecting herself from a body blow, but she didn't shy away.

I wanted to say more but bit my lip. What if she was right and her dad was only putting on a pretence? Advising her to give him a chance would only open her up to more pain. Her shoulders softened under my arm, and she leaned her head on my shoulder. Tears streamed down her face, and I rifled through my pocket and handed her a handkerchief. She sniffled as she took it, her lips curving into a small smile.

'You're my hero.'

Her gaze was full of something. I wanted nothing more than to lean down and kiss her. *Stop dreaming, James. She's just feeling vulnerable and needing a friend.*

I cleared my throat and lifted my arm off her shoulders. She sat up straight. I felt her looking at me but didn't look back, too scared that I'd misinterpret the look in her eyes yet again and fall under her spell.

Sabiha spent the rest of the day subdued and preoccupied. I wanted to check in on her but second-guessed myself. Would she think I was into her again? I erred on the side of caution and just remained in her orbit without asking questions.

***

I was working on my comic book when there was a knock on my window. I walked over and lifted the curtain, startled to find Sabiha standing below my bedroom window. 'Why didn't you come to the door?'

'I didn't want to freak out your Mum. It's kind of late-ish.'

I looked at the clock. It was after eight pm, not too late, but late for visitors. 'Meet me at the front door, and I'll let you in.'

She shook her head. 'No, I don't want your mum to know I'm here.' She looked around and climbed the fence, using the fence post to stand on my window ledge.

'What's going on?' I asked as I put my hands around her waist and helped her inside. She was wearing a t-shirt and pyjama pants. Her feet were bare and dirty, her eyes red-rimmed.

'I had to run away from home.' She wiped her face. 'Brian wasn't home, and I couldn't go to Dina because her parents would rat me out.'

I knew there had to be a reason she was at my window ledge by herself, but it still disappointed me I wasn't her first choice.

'Why did you run away?' Did her mum get sick again and act out, trying to hit her like last time?

'My dad showed up at my house.' She used her fingers to make quotation marks as she spoke about her father. 'My grandfather invited him and was talking to him in the living room. I knew he would make me talk to him, so I jumped out the window.' She was shivering. She'd run halfway across St Albans in bare feet and wearing only a t-shirt.

I got the blanket off my bed and wrapped her in it, sitting next to her and holding her tightly against me as she shivered. When she'd warmed up, I opened my wardrobe and got my jumper. She put it on, and I handed her socks. Her feet were dirty and callused.

'I'll get a first aid kit.'

'No, don't leave.' She held me tighter against her, looking at me plaintively.

I knew that the only reason she wanted me to is because her whole world had tilted on its axis and she was drowning in pain, but I still felt my breath hitch in my chest. 'I'll be right back. I just want to tend to your cut.'

'Don't tell anyone I'm here,' she said when I reached the door. 'I don't want anyone to find me.'

I nodded, glad to have a moment to gather myself. *She's not here for you, James,* I chastised myself. *She's only here because she needs somewhere to hide.* I went to the kitchen and got the first aid kit. I heard Sarah and Mum watching a reality TV show in the living room. They didn't pay attention as I got wipes and returned to my bedroom. I sat next to her and lifted her feet to my lap. Sabiha sat docile as I wiped her feet and then used antiseptic. She winced as I dabbed the scratches and then put a bandaid on the sole of her right foot. I got my warm socks, put them on her, and then tucked her under the covers.

'I can't go home tonight,' she whispered. 'I don't want them to know where I am.'

'What about your Mum? Won't she worry?'

'I called her from a payphone. Told her I was staying with a friend.' She looked at me with pleading in her eyes.

I hesitated, my body reacting at the thought of her in my bedroom all night. This wasn't a good idea. *Danger, danger, Will Robinson.* I heard the robotic voice from the TV show *Lost in Space* and knew I should say no, but I also knew I couldn't refuse her in her hour of need.

I cleared my throat. 'Sure, you can stay here.' My body reacted the minute I said the words, my blood rushing through my veins, and whooshing in my head. I had to keep my distance. 'I'll sleep in my sleeping bag on the floor,' I added.

'Thank you.' She snuggled further into my chest. My body reacted, and I had to fight the urge to nuzzle her neck, to lean down and kiss her. That's not what she was here for. Or should I make a move? She tilted her head up at me and I leaned down. Her eyes widened. Her body tensed, but she didn't move away. My lips were close to hers. She held her breath as she waited.

I wanted to kiss her, but something about how she held herself so tightly gave me pause. This wasn't the pose of a girl who wanted attention. I shifted, lifting her slightly off me as I tried to get my body to behave. Now wasn't the time. She was emotionally overwrought, and I couldn't be the sleaze bag friend who tried to come onto her. 'Do you want to watch a movie?' It was still too early to go to bed, and I desperately needed a buffer.

She nodded.

My desk was next to the bed, so I reached over and turned the computer to face us. 'Do you have any requests?'

'Something sad,' she said. 'I need a good cathartic cry.'

I flicked through the sentimental movies. The first one was *The Notebook*. My finger hesitated. We did not need to watch a romantic movie. I looked back at her. Or did we?

'Oooh, *Titanic*.' Her face lit up when she saw the screen icon.

I sighed and hit play. '*Titanic* it is.' Sabiha sat beside me on the bed, our arms hooked together, her hair draping my chest.

I couldn't concentrate on the screen, my whole body on alert, my skin on fire where we were pressed against each other. As I nuzzled her hair, breathing in the scent of vanilla, my body reacted. I shifted, relieved that the blanket was bunched over my lap as desire thrummed.

'I'll get us some snacks.' I broke in, needing a reprieve to clear my head. The impulse to make a move was becoming overwhelming. Sabiha sat up, and I got out of bed, going to the kitchen. I put the popcorn in the microwave and washed my face, needing to cool my head.

Sarah came in and looked questioningly at the two cans in my hand.

'I'm feeling thirsty.' My cheeks flushed, my tell that I was lying.

'You know, if I didn't know any better, I'd think you were hiding a girl in your room.'

I stared at the microwave as it whirred, my cheeks on fire, the tips of my ears hot.

'Jesse,' Sarah gasped and slapped me on the arm.

'It's not like that,' I whispered, shushing her. 'She can't go home tonight, so she's staying over.'

Sarah's eyes widened.

'Mum can't know.' I squeezed her arm warningly.

Sarah nodded, her lips pressed together as she stifled a giggle. 'I've got something for you.' She entered her bedroom and returned as I was tipping the popcorn into a bowl.

She handed me a foil packet. I pulled my fingers back, and it dropped to the ground as if it burnt. She bent and picked it up, putting it in my hand, making me clasp my fingers around it. 'Better safe than sorry.'

I tried to give it back to her.

'Take it, or I'll tell Mum.'

I stiffened and put it in the pocket of my jeans.

'You're welcome,' she called out as I stomped down the hallway with the bowl and cans.

I paused at the bathroom door and quickly entered, placing the popcorn and cans down as I fished the condoms out of my pocket to put them in the drawer. If entered the bedroom with them on me, I'd look shamefaced and guilty, and Sabiha would know I was up to something. Anyway, there was no way we were going to do anything. The most I wanted was a kiss, or a hug, or… My mind wandered, and I hesitated. Maybe I should keep them just in case. I tucked them in the back pocket of my jeans and went to my bedroom.

Sabiha was standing near my desk, looking at the pages of the graphic novel *Flesh and Love*. 'These are amazing.'

'Charlie's very talented.' I closed the door behind me and put down the popcorn and cans, hiding my face. I was caught between anticipation and agony as I waited for her to ask for more. I wanted nothing more than to tell her about the graphic book, but warred with Charlie's request for confidentiality and my trepidation that she would read it and freak out when she realised she was Sapphire.

She turned around and took a handful of popcorn. 'Yum.' She sat back on the bed and glanced up at me, waiting for me to sit.

I followed her lead and sat next to her. We had our backs against the headboard, and I was relieved that the popcorn bowl acted like a buffer. We munched on popcorn and drank the sodas, murmuring comments about the movie.

When it finished, it was close to midnight, and I blinked blearily.

Sabiha shifted uncomfortably. 'Is it safe for me to use the bathroom?'

'Yeah, Sarah and Mum are in bed.' I opened my bedroom and checked the hallway.

She tiptoed out. While she was gone, I set up my sleeping bag on the floor with my pillows and took my pyjamas out. When she returned, she looked at the sleeping bag on the floor with something like disappointment. Had I made a mistake? Should

I have used this opportunity so that we could sleep together with her in the same bed? No, that way, madness lies. We were friends, and this was not the time for something more.

I took my pyjamas and went to the bathroom, brushing my teeth and changing. When I returned, Sabiha was lying in my bed, her hand under her cheek, her face turned toward the door. I wanted to kiss her lips, found myself moving toward the bed like a magnet. She opened her eyes, and I realised I was standing above her. She flinched before collecting herself.

Damn it, James. You're acting like a stalker. 'Sorry,' I muttered.

'No, it's fine. I'm sorry.' She reached her hand and took mine. 'Thank you for being there for me.'

'Sure.' I tugged her hand away from mine and sat on the sleeping bag.

'I don't know what I'd do without you,' Sabiha said softly, a tear glistening in her eye.

'You never need to find out.' I switched off the lamp abruptly, needing to cut the visual of her in my bed before I did something I would regret. I lay down in my sleeping bag. 'Good night, Sabiha,' I whispered into the darkness.

'Good night, Jesse.' I felt her hand on my shoulder as she reached for me.

I moved closer to the bed and held her hand, listening to her breathing even out as she fell asleep. I held her hand long after it went limp, not wanting to give up touching her.

The bright sun hit my face and woke me. I opened my eyes and saw Sabiha lying on the edge of the bed, in the position she had fallen asleep, her hand hanging off the side of the bed. I watched her sleep in wonder, happiness suffusing me. Her eyes fluttered open, and she met mine. There was a moment of confusion on her face before it cleared, and she smiled with joy.

I couldn't help it. I sat up on the floor and reached for her, my head bending toward hers. Suddenly her eyes flickered closed, and her lips pressed together as she held herself stiffly. Shit, I'd misread the situation again. There was a thud, and I sprung away, filled with relief.

'Wake up Jesse,' Sarah shouted, giving my door one more bang for measure.

'Sorry, just my sister waking me up.' I mussed my hair nervously. Sabiha didn't need to know that Sarah never woke me up, and the only reason she was doing it today was to give me a heads up to get Sabiha to leave before Mum awoke.

Sabiha nodded, looking embarrassed. 'I should probably get home before Mum freaks out.' She pushed the doona off her. She stood, looking at her pyjama in dismay as she crossed her arms over her thin t-shirt.

'I'll lend you some clothes.' I went to my wardrobe and handed her grey tracksuit pants and bottom. 'You change here, and I'll change in the bathroom.' I took my jeans and jumper and left the bedroom.

Sarah was lying in wait in the kitchen doorway. Her eyebrows waggled. 'So?'

'So, nothing!' I stomped past her and went into the bathroom. Why did I keep making the same mistake? I had to learn once and for all that she thought of me as a friend. That's it.

I approached my door and softly knocked. Sabiha opened it, peering out shyly, my tracksuit hanging off her. 'Do you want to go to McDonald's for breakfast before I go home?' she asked.

I hesitated. I thought she'd try to run off like the hounds of hell were on her tail. Instead, she wanted us to spend more time together? She probably just wanted to avoid going home and dealing with her grandfather and mother.

'Sure.'

I helped her out the window and went through the house and to the front door, meeting her on the street. We were walking down the street when someone shouted my name. I turned and saw Brian. He was wearing jeans and a singlet, looking worse for the wear with a droopy smile on his face.

'Oooh, the walk of shame?' He gaped at us.

'What? No!' Sabiha looked uncharacteristically nervous, biting on her thumbnail. 'My dad showed up, and I needed to hide out.'

'Sorry.' Brian enveloped her in a hug.

'We're going to Maccas—' she interrupted, trying to move things along.

'Fuck yes, Maccas run.' Brian inserted himself between us, throwing his arm around our shoulders, and we lurched down the street as he leaned on us.

I thought I saw a flicker of disappointment on Sabiha's face that Brian was three-wheeling, but I must have imagined it. She didn't really want to spend more time alone with me?

'Rough night?' I asked Brian, arching an eyebrow.

'Rough, but good.' He smiled suggestively.

I smiled despite myself. I needed to stop fighting my fate and accept the signs from the universe—Sabiha and I weren't meant to be anything but friends.

Chapter 14

'Everyone, settle,' Ms Partridge called out as a young girl with Sabiha's face followed her into class, wearing jeans pants and a white shirt.

I glanced at Sabiha, on edge, like I was waiting for a volcano to explode. Since Sabiha's father showed up a few months ago, the Sassy Saints had all done our best to avoid the topic. Sabiha struggled with tension at home and her mother's recovery, having good and bad days. The good days were when she was bright and sparkly. The bad when depression took her under, and she slinked into school like a shadow.

We'd settled into friendship once more, and she didn't seem to notice any simmering tension because of my attraction, so I'd tried to tamp down my feelings again. Now, as I glanced between her and the new student, I felt that things were about to get interesting again.

'This is our new student Alma Omerović.' Ms Partridge's forehead wrinkled for a moment, and she looked at the back. 'Are you any relation to Sabiha?' she asked.

Time stopped as Alma followed Ms Partridge's gaze and met Sabiha's eyes.

Sabiha's face darkened with rage. 'No,' Sabiha spat out, breaking the spell. 'We're not related.'

Alma looked like she was going to bolt for the door, her eyes wide with fright. My heart broke for her. I knew Sabiha felt betrayed about her dad, but taking it out on her sister wasn't fair.

'You can sit next to Dina,' Ms Partridge continued, oblivious to the tension in the air.

Sabiha stood and collected her things, her resentment obvious as she slammed her notebook and slapped her pencil case together. She looked like a girl lumberjack; she wore a denim mini and pink leggings, and her feet were encased in chunky worker boots.

'Sabiha, quiet.' The teacher shushed.

Sabiha moved to an empty desk in the last row behind us. 'Are you okay?' Brian asked.

'Not now.' She shook her head.

I could tell she was fighting back tears, masking her emotions with anger. We turned around and left her, knowing that nothing could be done when she was in such a volatile state of mind.

Alma slid into the seat next to Dina. 'Hi,' she whispered, trying to make eye contact, but Dina snubbed her.

Both girls had the same miserable expression as they avoided looking at each other. It was disconcerting, like watching a movie on a slow internet connection where the buffering made it slow-motion. They repeated the same gestures a few minutes after each other.

After English double period, the recess bell rang, and Alma turned to catch Sabiha madly packing her things to dash for the door.

'Can we talk?' She followed Sabiha.

'About what?' Sabiha whirled around. 'How your mother is a home wrecker?'

'No,' Alma stuttered to a stop. 'My Mum isn't—'

'Then how do you explain that we're the same age?' Sabiha snapped, turning around again.

The class emptied, and only the Sassy Saints and Alma were left.

'We're not the same age,' Alma shouted.

Sabiha stopped, turning around again, her mouth open to continue her tirade.

'I'm a year younger,' Alma continued quietly, since Sabiha was listening. 'I was moved up a grade in primary school.'

Sabiha looked at her suspiciously like she wasn't sure whether or not to believe Alma.

'It's true,' Alma insisted and shared her birthday.

Sabiha's gaze softened, and she looked off-kilter and lost. I wanted to take her in my arms and comfort her.

'You okay?' Dina put her arm around Sabiha's shoulders.

'I can't do this,' Sabiha muttered and rushed off.

I hesitated, looking back at Alma with an apology in my eyes, but followed as the Sassy Saints all left the room. While I felt an inexplicable sense of connection to Alma because of her resemblance to Alma, it was Sabiha who I owed my loyalty to.

As we walked out, we huddled around the front bench.

'Did you see how much she looked like me? She could be my twin.' Sabiha shivered, like she was in shock.

I moved to stand next to her, and before I had time to second-guess, I put my arm around her and held her tightly against me. She turned her head into my shoulder and cried. Brian and Dina looked at each other with concern as I rubbed Sabiha's back to soothe her. Sabiha was not prone to emotional displays that were not anger. We were all at a loss about how to handle it.

'It will be okay,' I murmured, hoping I was right.

Sabiha stopped crying, lifting her head as she shuddered to a halt. 'Did you know?' she asked Dina.

Since the two of them were Bosnian, their families were in each other's orbit socially.

'No, I did not know you had a doppelgänger.' Dina lifted her hands in denial. 'If I did, I would have told you.'

Sabiha wasn't crying anymore, but she didn't move away from my arms. I loosely held them around her, and she had her arm around my waist.

'I didn't know what my father looks like,' she said softly.

The Sassy Saints looked at each other in shock.

'What do you mean?' Dina clarified, moving closer. 'He's been in Melbourne for a few months now.'

'I wouldn't meet with him.' Sabiha's jaw set in defiance. 'He abandoned me. Now I was abandoning him.'

'I bet you're regretting that decision now,' Brian muttered.

Sabiha glared at him briefly before looking defeated again. 'I only have the one blurry photo in Mum's photo alum. She always said I was his spitting image, and I guess she wasn't exaggerating.' She rubbed her eye and tried to laugh, but it came out choked.

'You know you have other siblings,' Dina said hesitantly, as if she was scared of Sabiha's reaction. 'I haven't met them or anything. I just know because of the Bosnian telegraph. A brother and another sister.'

Sabiha winced. 'Shit. That's a lot to deal with. I've been an only child all my life, and now I'm tripping over siblings.' She rubbed her face in frustration. 'What am I going to do? Alma's here now, and I have to see her every day. My reminder of all the things I want to forget.'

'You don't have to do anything now,' I said, remembering my coping strategies during Mum's hard days of cancer. 'You just have to get through today.'

Sabiha nodded shakily. Dina took her to the bathroom to wash her face.

'Fuck, that's a lot to handle.' Brian rubbed his neck after they left.

'Yep.' I nodded.

Sabiha was subdued for the rest of the day, slightly shell-shocked and dazed. We ran interference for her, and Dina walked home with her, saying she would get her mum to pick her up from Sabiha's house. I was glad that she was going to be there for her.

***

The next day Alma was in our class for the first two periods. She arrived early and sat at the back of the class. We sat close to the windows in the middle of the classroom, so she was behind us. Sabiha kept her gaze on the front of the classroom, her back ramrod straight as she fought the urge to look back.

I glanced back, once catching Alma's glance. She looked so sad that I mustered a smile in her direction. Her lips quirked slightly, but she couldn't quite muster a full smile. For the rest of the week, it became the norm to see Alma walking down the corridor by herself.

'Maybe we should ask her to hang around with us?' I said at lunchtime, as we saw Alma through the library window perusing the shelves. 'She is your sister, after all.'

'In name only,' Sabiha said venomously. 'She's nothing to me.' She stared broodily at Alma.

'It's not her fault,' I waded in. 'Your father and mother made these decisions. It's not fair to blame Alma.'

Sabiha shot me a look of betrayal and shifted away from me, giving me the cold shoulder. I bit back any advice I had in the future. I didn't know how she could be so cruel, but I tried to tell myself it wasn't fair to judge her. After all, how would I feel if a secret brother popped out of the woodwork and was at my school, under my nose every day?

I caught sight of a blonde hair and looked to see Alma walking past us with Alex Payne. Dina saw too, and nudged Sabiha to look. I followed them and saw he was headed to the school side gate leading to what everyone called Blow Job lane.

I ran back to Sabiha, out of breath. 'You have to do something. You can't let him take her out to that lane.'

'Why?' Sabiha demanded, her hand fisting by her side. 'She's not my problem.'

'So what? She's someone who needs help.' I held my hand out in the direction they went. 'You know what Alex is like and what he will expect. You can't let Alma walk into that.'

Sabiha looked militant.

'Sabiha, we have to help her,' Dina said gently. 'She's an innocent girl, and Alex is a predator.'

Sabiha took a shuddering sigh and nodded. 'Fine.'

I breathed a sigh of relief as they ran after Alma. If Sabiha hadn't done it, I don't know that I could have forgiven her for being that coldhearted.

'Well, that's a plot twist,' Brian said wryly. 'Big sister to the rescue. I didn't think Sabiha had it in her.'

'Don't be an asshole. Sabiha has a heart.'

'Maybe.' Brian shrugged.

We walked over and joined the girls.

'So we're welcoming the prodigal sister into the fold,' Brian said. 'Introductions are in order. I'm Brian.' He offered his hand.

Alma looked at him with suspicion. He looked like he was impersonating a hobo. His hair hadn't seen a comb in a week, and his clothes were creased like he wore them to bed.

'This is Jesse.' Brian jerked his head to me, and I smiled weakly.

'And I believe you know Dina.'

Alma gave Dina a dirty look. It had been Dina's duty to take Alma under her wing as the resident Bosnian ambassador, and she'd failed. Dina had the grace to look guilty.

'You're Sabiha's little sister.' Brian said.

'Step sister,' Sabiha snapped.

'Half-sister,' Alma corrected. 'Same father, different mothers.'

'We're not real sisters, though,' Sabiha said, scoring the first point.

'Of course not,' Alma replied calmly. 'I already have one of each and don't need anymore.'

Sabiha was surprised, and I smothered a smile as I realised the resemblance was more than skin deep.

'Burn,' Brian interrupted before Sabiha rallied. 'I see the bitchy gene is hereditary.'

'Shut up.' Sabiha pushed him.

Brian dropped his diary, and Alma bent to pick it up. She paused with an outreached hand when she saw the collage of male movie stars on his cover, most bare-chested, with their pecs glistening. She slowly handed the diary to Brian.

'As you can see, I'm partial to blondes,' Brian hammed it up, lisping slightly.

She forced a smile, looking uncomfortable.

A chill settled on my skin. If she were a homophobe, things would not end well. Sabiha would rip her to shreds, and that would be just the beginning. Thankfully, Sabiha didn't notice her pause.

Sabiha began walking, and we followed.

'Are you coming?' Brian asked Alma.

Sabiha slowed her steps, waiting for my answer.

'I've got things to do,' Alma said.

'Nonsense,' I spoke for the first time. 'We'd be delighted for you to join us.' I had to make sure we accepted Alma as part of the group. It was the only way Sabiha would accept her newfound sister and reconnect with her father.

Alma waited to see if Sabiha would protest.

'Hurry, I'm starving,' Sabiha snapped over her shoulder.

Alma joined us.

'We'll give you a tour of the school,' Dina said.

We walked through the school grounds, and Dina pointed out buildings. There was an awkward silence between Dina's commentary as if no one could think of what to say.

'I thought they enrolled you at Searers College?' Dina asked.

'I was,' Alma replied. 'But my parents decided it wasn't the right environment for me. They thought I needed more academic opportunities.'

Dina looked confused. 'I thought they expelled you,' she blurted out.

'Um, well—' Alma stuttered. 'Yes, I was,' she admitted, her cheeks flushed.

'Way to go,' Brian said, putting his arm around Alma's shoulders.

'But it's not a bad thing,' Dina protested. 'See.' She reached into her backpack and pulled out a newspaper article.

Alma looked away while we huddled around. Alma had written about her anti-Muslim teacher at the school, her prose scathing. She was a natural writer. I looked at Sabiha to see how she responded to all the similarities between her and her sister.

She looked like she'd swallowed a lemon. 'Ever heard of the saying, "don't shit where you eat?"' Sabiha said deadpan.

'I didn't think you were the type of person who'd side with the uneducated masses,' I said.

'I'm not,' Sabiha looked flustered. 'But sometimes you have to pick your battles.'

'And sometimes you have to stand for something.' I shrugged. Why was she so determined to put down Alma, even when she was clearly displaying honourable qualities?

'I didn't do it alone,' Alma interrupted. 'A friend helped.'

The tension between Sabiha and me dissipated.

'Of course you did,' Sabiha said. 'You don't look like the type who could do anything alone.'

Alma gasped.

I looked at her with an accusatory look. She was being such a bitch.

'What?' snapped at me before storming off in a fury.

'Sorry,' Dina muttered and went to catch up with her.

'Don't worry.' I put my hand on Alma's shoulder. 'She'll come around. After all, you are sisters.'

Alma forced a smile and nodded, looking like she didn't believe me. I couldn't let on I doubted it myself. I would have thought Sabiha would have softened by now. Instead, she was digging her heels in more.

'You'd better be careful about taking Alma's side. Sabiha is an only child and she doesn't deal with sharing,' Brian cautioned as we followed the girls.

'You know she's doing the wrong thing. Are we just supposed to let it slide?'

Brian nodded. 'Yes, we are.'

A lump of anger lodged in my throat. I couldn't stand injustice and unfairness, and Sabiha was displaying both. Was I supposed to give up my morals for Sabiha's approval?

Sabiha determinedly avoided my gaze when we joined them and didn't speak directly to me while Dina nervously watched on. I was chastened, but then my anger built as the day passed.

'Are you seriously giving me the silent treatment?' I burst out as we walked out of our last class.

Dina and Brian were each beside us, and I saw them nervously step back as I confronted Sabiha.

'You're supposed to be my friend,' Sabiha said, sounding petulant.

'I am your friend.' I gritted my teeth. 'And being friends doesn't mean I can't tell you when you're wrong. So let me be clear, you're wrong. The way you're treating Alma is deplorable and I will not stand by and watch anymore. Either she's one of the Sassy Saints, or I'm out.'

Sabiha gasped, her cheeks flushing red with rage.

Brian stamped forward. 'Yeah, I have to agree. I know it's hard for you, but it's also really hard to watch the way you talk to her.' He glared at Dina.

Dina reluctantly stepped forward. 'And my mum is going to give me grief if I don't shepherd Alma around. She's already been asking me about her every day.'

Sabiha looked militant as she stared at us all, her hands fisted by her sides. She took a deep breath, tamping down her rage. 'Fine. She's in.'

She turned on her heel and stalked off. Dina followed, giving Brian the finger.

'See, I got your back, brah.' Brian put his arm around my comma *shoulders,* and we walked to the lockers. 'You can thank me by doing my English homework.'

I glared at him.

'Okay, I'll settle for seeing your notes.'

I knew he'd intervened to stop a confrontation between me and Sabiha, but I wished he hadn't. I'd been tiptoeing around her for so long, desperate for her approval and I was getting sick of the friendship limbo. Did she really care about me, or would she let me go?

Chapter 15

Brian was lying on my bed listlessly, flicking through my notebooks as I sat at my desk on my computer.

'You're going to have to do some homework,' I told him.

He didn't look at me.

'Unless you want to fail and work in construction.'

He gave me a cranky side-eye, before sitting up and writing notes in his notebook.

He'd been so depressed and lacklustre since Adnan dumped him. It was like he was on a direct route to self-sabotage. The only reason he came over now was to avoid his father.

I turned back to my graphic novel. My email notifications pinged, and I flicked my screen. An email from Gordonio. I felt a flutter in my stomach and told myself not to be silly. I opened the email and read. It took a moment for the words to hit my synapsis and for me to decipher.

'We would like to make you and Charlie Lacertosa a publishing contract for your graphic novel *Flesh and Love*.' I skimmed through the rest of the email, noticing that they'd copied Charlie in and that there was an attachment below.

I gasped, my stomach lurching. I couldn't believe this had happened.

'What is? Are you okay?' Brian asked.

I couldn't speak, just pointed to the screen. Brian stood and leaned forward, reading over my shoulder. 'OMG, your book is going to be published.' Brian jumped in place, slapping me on the shoulder.

'My book is going to be published,' I repeated, the truth settling on me. It was actually going to happen. My dream was going to come true. 'My book is going to get published,' I said again, my voice stronger as happiness hit.

'Your book is going to get published,' Brian shouted and started cheering.

'Jesse, Jesse,' I heard Sarah's voice down the hall. She opened the door without knocking. 'Are you okay?'

'My book is going to get published,' I told her.

Her eyes widened. 'What?'

Brian pointed to my computer screen. She squinted as she read without her glasses. 'OMG. Your book is going to get published.' She hugged me tightly, laughing and crying. 'Mama, Mama.' She ran down the hall screaming to mum. She returned, wheeling her down the hallway.

Mum's blue eyes glistened with tears, her face wreathed in a smile. 'I'm so proud of you, my son.' She held up her hands, and I knelt at her feet and wrapped my arms around her. She hugged me tight, stroking my hair as I leaned on her shoulder. Sarah leaned forward and hugged me too. The three of us intertwined around Mum's wheelchair.

Brian stood back, crossing his arms over his waist, looking lost. I lifted my arm, waving him forward and pulled him into the huddle.

'I thought you'd never ask,' he murmured against my back as he hugged me from behind.

I snort-laughed, and he grinned. We pulled apart.

'We need to celebrate,' Sarah said. 'To the kitchen.' She wheeled Mum, and Brian and I followed. 'I think this is an occasion for an ice cream sundae.'

'I'll be there in a minute. I need to call Charlie.' Even though he'd been copied in the email, he probably hadn't seen it. He forgot to check his email for weeks at a time.

Charlie answered, not speaking, just waiting, as was his phone manner. 'Charlie, check your emails.'

'Okay,' Charlie said.

I heard the clicking of the keyboard, and then a slight puff of air hit the receiver, Charlie's version of a gasp.

'We're going to be published authors,' I exclaimed.

'Okay.' Charlie said, his voice its usual monotone.

'We did it. All that hard work pitching paid off. We got our dream publisher, Gordonio.'

'We did.' Charlie paused. 'We'll have to check the contract clauses before we sign. I'm not falling for the Superman clause.'

'I don't think they have that anymore.' Charlie was obsessed with comic books, and the creator of Superman sold his ideas, including the characters. He didn't get any money each time they made a new version.

'Show the email to your parents,' I told him.

'Okay.' Charlie replied.

'I'll draft an email of acceptance for you to look at before I send.' We hung up.

Even though Charlie sounded as if he couldn't care less, I knew he was just as excited as me.

I entered the kitchen, my mouth watering as I opened the cupboard and took out the narrow boat dishes we used for sundaes. Sarah took out the ice cream from the freezer while Brian got bananas from the fruit bowl and began peeling them. This was a ritual we had completed once or twice. Within five minutes, they finished the sundaes, and Sarah placed the maraschino cherry on top. We sat with a spoon, and I scooped the ice cream smothered in chocolate sauce; I moaned as it hit my tongue.

'Okay, now tell us about this book you wrote and how it came about that you're getting published?' Sarah demanded, slapping her hands on the table.

'Yeah, I want the details too,' Brian said.

I laughed and told them about the literary speed dating that I'd kept on the down-low.

'You dark horse.' Brian slapped my shoulder. 'How did Charlie react?'

'He's happy.' I scooped my ice cream.

Brian took his cherry and slurped it down. 'It's going to do so much for my cred having a published author as a friend.'

I smiled faintly. Of course, Brian would think about how it would affect him.

'When's the book launch? I need to plan the most fabulous outfit.' He took another spoon. 'All the Sassy Saints should come.'

'Who are the Sassy Saints?' Mum asked.

'Me, Jesse, Sabiha, Alma and Dina.'

There was one name that Brian omitted from that list—Adnan. Even though he wasn't an official member, I still thought of him as an honorary.

I wondered how Sabiha was going to react. I felt like calling to tell her but tamped down the urge. It would be more thrilling to tell her in person and see her reaction.

'Sabiha is going to lose her mind,' Brian said.

I sat up, wondering if I'd said something aloud as I daydreamed about her reaction. No one was looking at me weirdly.

'Are you going to call her?' he asked.

I shook my head. 'I want to tell her in person.'

Brian winked and nodded. 'You sly dog. You know, we should prepare you properly for your big announcement.'

'What do you mean?' I asked.

'I mean, you need to re-think your look now that you're going to be a man of the people.'

'Yes,' Sarah clutched my arm. 'You need to get a makeover.'

'You want to look your best when you tell everyone your big news,' Mum chimed in.

'I'm going to go home and get supplies.' Brian quickly spooned the last of his sundae in his mouth.

'What supplies?' I asked.

'Your wardrobe is more on the hobo chic side. We need to glow you up.' Brian ran out the front door without waiting for a response.

'I'm going to regret this,' I muttered.

'No, you won't.' Sarah kissed me on the cheek. 'Now is your time. You need to embrace it.'

My phone rang, and I saw it was Charlie's mother, Martha. 'Is it true?' she asked when I answered. 'The comic book you and Charlie did together is going to be published.'

'Yes, it's true.'

'I didn't know you and Charlie were working on a book together. I just thought you were mucking about.'

'We were. We were doing what we loved, and then I saw the opportunity and asked Charlie about submitting, and well, here we are.' I stuttered to a stop, the reality hitting me again. My writing was going to get published. My book would be published. It was something I had barely let myself imagine or dream about.

'How is Charlie taking it?' I asked.

'He's okay,' Martha said, sounding unsure. 'He's just playing a computer game.'

We both knew this was his coping strategy when he was feeling overwhelmed.

'Well, congratulations. And thank you for everything.' Martha sounded choked up. 'You're a wonderful friend to Charlie.'

'He's a great friend to me,' I replied. I knew she acknowledged few people saw past Charlie's oddness to the cool kid he was, but I also hated the way they made it out that I was doing something so altruistic by being friends with him. Charlie was a friend because I enjoyed spending time with him. He was the only person who shared my love of graphic novels and writing. I loved being in his company because he just accepted me, without needing to talk or explain. We vibed off each other well.

As I hung up, I heard the doorbell ring. I walked to the front door and opened it. Brian was wincing in pain, coat hangers hanging off his arms while he held bags in his hands.

'Did you bring your entire wardrobe?' I unhooked the coat hangers and carried them ahead.

'There's a lot of work to do.' Brian followed me to my bedroom and placed the bags on the floor. 'First, the outfit.' He held up black pleated pants and a blue velvet shirt.

'I'm not a pimp.' I sat on the office chair facing him.

'This isn't a pimp outfit.'

I lifted an eyebrow.

He looked back at the outfit and threw it on the bed. 'Business chic.' He held up grey flannel pants with a white shirt. 'And this is for a writerly touch.' He held up black suspenders.

'Mmm, that would be a suitable outfit for the book launch.'

'Good choice. We'll put that one in your wardrobe for then.' Brian opened my wardrobe and placed them inside. 'We're looking for an outfit for tomorrow. For your big debut as an author at the school.' He lifted black silk pants and a purple t-shirt with rhinestones on it.

'Seriously? Have you met me?'

'Fine. So you just want to wear a t-shirt and jeans then.'

'Yes, that would be perfect.'

Brian's eyes narrowed. 'Okay. I'll be right back.' He ran back out the door.

Sarah popped her head in. 'How's the makeover going?'

'We are in the perusing stage.' I gestured toward the clothes piled on the bed.

Sarah stifled a grin. 'I can't wait to see what you end up wearing.' She entered and lifted another shirt, this one silver with pimp daddy in pink glitter on it.

'It will definitely be none of those.'

Brian ran back into the house, his face flushed and perspiration on his forehead. 'I found it.' He held up a pair of whitewashed jeans and a white t-shirt.

I took them from him and held them up against myself. 'These look tight.'

'So? They're going to fit. Try them on.'

I looked at Sarah for help. 'Yes, try them on.'

'Fine.' I gestured for them to leave.

I removed my tracksuit pants and daggy t-shirt and pulled up the jeans. They felt uncomfortably tight. My jeans were always loose-fitting that billowed slightly when I walked. I'd never worn jeans that were fitted against my body. I pulled on the white t-shirt. It was tight, too. I yanked at the collar, trying to pull it away from my neck as I opened the door. 'I don't think this is going to work.'

'Wow, you're a hunk.' Brian looked me up and down, checking me out.

'He's not wrong. How did this happen?' Sarah squeezed my biceps. 'You look amazing.'

'It's not me. It feels uncomfortable.' I walked around. The jeans were already softening around my body. Still, it felt weird.

'See yourself.' Sarah took my arm and yanked me to her bedroom. She pushed me in front of the full-length mirror on her wall.

I turned and looked at myself. It was like I was looking at a trick mirror for a moment. I was so used to seeing myself as the pudgy kid, with doughy arms and stomach, that I couldn't process the image before me. The t-shirt fitted around my torso, showing off my wide shoulders. The cuffs stretched around my biceps, making them look bulging. And the jeans moulded against my legs so they looked thin and long. It was like I was someone else. Someone cool. I straightened, looking closer at myself. It was a new me.

'Can you imagine Sabiha's face when she sees you in that outfit?' Brian peered over my shoulder, and I met his eyes. He was looking at me with admiration. It was the first time I'd seen myself in this way. I wanted so desperately to see Sabiha looking at me like this.

'Alright. I'll wear it tomorrow.'

'Attaboy.' Brian lifted his hand, and we high-fived. 'Now we need to style your hair.'

'What?' I ran my hands through my hair. 'It's fine.'

Brian yanked my elbow and led me back to my bedroom.

'No, it's really not.' Sarah followed.

'Get changed, and we'll try some different styles.' Brian pushed me in and closed the bedroom door.

I got back into my comfy trackies. The next hour I spent in the bathroom as Brian smoothed my hair with many hair products, brushing it this way and that, using a blow-dryer. He and Sarah conferred about which one was best while I sat mutely.

'This one works, but I need to trim it.' Brian finger-combed my hair.

'You? Cut my hair. No.' I shook my head.

'Who do you think cuts my hair?' Brian shook his brown locks.

'Really?'

'Really?'

Brian opened one bag and produced a black gown that he draped around me and scissors. I bit my lip as he snipped. He put hair product through again and then a blow-dryer. 'This is the one.'

He and Sarah nodded approvingly. I stood and looked in the mirror. The sides of my hair were close-shaven, the top curling back and slightly mussed.

'I'm never going to do this myself.' I turned from side to side, admiring the way it sat.

'That's okay. I'll come by early and recreate it tomorrow and teach you how to do it yourself, under my supervision.'

Brian packed up, and I walked him home, helping carry back all his accessories.

'I'll return the jeans and t-shirt after I wash them.' I held out the coat hangers, and Brian carefully put them back in his wardrobe, organising them by colour and style.

Brian shook his head. 'Keep them. They're my present to you.'

'They're expensive. Too expensive.'

'I don't care. They're yours.' Brian closed the wardrobe door. 'Tomorrow, your life is going to change forever. Just promise me it won't all go to your head and you'll drop me.'

'I would never do that. You're my best friend. Forever.' I hugged him, holding him tight. 'You're the one who's known me through it all. You're my one true friend.'

Brian's eyes were glistening. 'You're my true friend, too.'

'Good.' I patted him on the back. 'Don't forget to come early. You need to make me look all spunky.'

Brian laughed. 'You're already getting so vain.'

I laughed too. He walked me out.

As I walked home, I revelled in the night's quiet. Was Brian right? Was this going to change my life forever? I shivered, partly in excitement and partly in trepidation. Either way, the next few weeks were going to be something.

'You ready?' Brian asked as we neared the school gates.

I nodded, swallowing rapidly.

Brian bounced as he walked. We turned into the school. I searched for Sabiha's blonde hair. She was standing between Dina and Alma. Alma was looking at me with surprise. I saw the moment that Dina and Sabiha turned. As we approached, their eyes widened in surprise.

I felt self-conscious again, wondering if I'd made a mistake wearing these jeans and t-shirt. I shouldn't have let Brian talk me into this.

'Jesse?' Sabiha said questioningly when I was nearer.

There was more than surprise in her gaze. She was checking me out, her eyes glancing at my biceps and chest. I straightened my back. She was seeing me as a man.

'What's going on?' Sabiha asked.

'Do you like?' Brian almost danced on tiptoes. 'I did a makeover,' he screeched.

My cheeks turned pink under their attention.

'Tell them.' Brian slapped my shoulder.

I took a deep breath. 'My book is getting published.'

My announcement dropped to the ground like a lead balloon.

'Wow, congratulations.' Alma jumped into the silence after it stretched out too long.

'What book?' Sabiha demanded.

'I've been writing a graphic novel with my friend, Charlie. You know, the artist. Anyway, we met a publisher at a Writer's Centre event, and he requested we submit and...' I held my hands up.

'I didn't know you were writing a book,' Sabiha snapped.

Was she angry at me? 'We weren't exactly on speaking terms,' I replied softly.

Sabiha looked away, blinking rapidly.

'That's amazing news.' Dina pushed past Sabiha and hugged me.

'That's my boy.' Brian slapped him on the arm. 'Tell them the plot.'

As I told them about the plot, Sabiha softened, oohing and aahing at the appropriate moments, her waspishness gone.

Brian and Dina separated and began talking to each other about their favourite music and exchanging the CDs they'd burnt. Sabiha, Alma, and I stood awkwardly for a moment, not knowing what to say to each other.

'I didn't have time to talk to you about your article the other day,' I said to Alma, flashing back to when we'd looked at the article that had her expelled from school. 'You're a talented writer. Maybe we can exchange work. Do you write fiction?'

'Um, no, not really.' Alma pushed her hair behind her ear and looked down.

'You're obviously talented. Isn't she Sabiha?' I glanced at Sabiha, forcing her to engage in the conversation.

'I guess,' Sabiha said grudgingly.

'Writing talent runs in the family.' Even though the two sisters had only recently met each other, they were so much alike. They just needed a nudge to see it.

Alma and Sabiha looked at each other with identical looks of scorn. Sabiha turned to me. 'So, when can I read your masterpiece?'

'I'll email it to you.' I went to run my hands through my hair but remembered Brian's effort in styling this morning just in time and stopped.

'Great.'

Sabiha smiled, and my heart fluttered. Not again. 'I'll email you a copy too, Alma,' I said, needing to downplay my feelings.

Sabiha's smile curdled on her face.

'Have you always wanted to write?' Alma asked me.

I nodded. 'Ever since I can remember. What about you? What do you want to be when you grow up?'

'A lawyer.'

'Really.' I frowned. 'Surprising. What's your passion?'

Alma paused. 'I guess reading,' she finally answered.

'I knew it.' I smiled. 'A love of reading is the first symptom of being a writer.'

Sabiha looked sour. The locker bell rang.

'What have you got next?' I asked as Alma examined the timetable at my locker. I wasn't gong to let Sabiha influence me in sidelining Alma any longer.

'Home Ec.' Alma looked at the map in her diary.

'I'm going that way.' I gestured for me to go ahead through the crowd while Sabiha receded in the background. 'Sabiha can come across as strong, but she has a soft side,' I continued when we got out onto the walkway. It was my chance to try and smooth it over between the two sisters.

'I hope you're right.'

'I am. It's been hard on her for the past few months. Suddenly having a father and finding out about this whole other family.'

Alma blinked rapidly, and I wanted to kick myself for being insensitive. 'But I'm sure it hasn't been easy on you either. I'm sorry.'

'It's okay.' Alma leaned her head forward so her hair shielded her face, but she still sounded choked up.

'No, it's not.' I put an arm on my shoulder and stepped in front of her. 'Sabiha wants to get to know you. She's just scared about opening herself up. Give her time.'

Alma's eyes cleared, and she flashed a smile. 'I'm sure you're right. I'd better hurry to class.'

I nodded in relief and stepped aside. Crisis averted. 'It's through those doors and to the left.' I pointed.

'Thanks.'

I turned back and headed to class. I sat at my desk and opened my computer while I waited for the teacher. I drafted a quick email and added Alma and Sabiha's email addresses. Quickly, before I could change my mind, I attached the draft of my graphic novel and hit send. Butterflies hit. What would happen when Sabiha read about her alter-ego?

Chapter 16

At the end of the day, I was at my locker when Sabiha approached. 'OMG Jesse. It's amazing.' Her eyes gleamed with excitement. 'Your book. I read your book.'

I gaped at her in amazement. 'I just sent it to you this morning.'

'Yeah, I was reading in class, just flicking between screens, when the teacher passed by. I had to read it all. I love Jasper. He is so beautiful and forgiving of Saphire's harshness.' She sighed, her face dreamy as she spoke about my alter-ego.

'Really.' I smiled, bemused. 'So you think Saphire is harsh?'

'Yeah. She's a right royal bitch. I mean, she gets redeemed in the end, but the shit she pulls on Jasper. I would have kicked her arse to the curb.' Her face scrunched up in frustration as she mimicked a kick.

Brian glanced at me over Sabiha's shoulder. His shoulders were shaking with laughter. Sabiha's hadn't picked up on Saphire being inspired by her.

A bark of laughter escaped me, even though I was fighting hard not to lose it.

Sabiha looked at me in confusion. 'What? You don't think she's a bitch.'

I wiped the smile off my face. 'She's my creation, so I'm always going to have a soft spot for her, but I love hearing what readers think of her.'

'See you tomorrow.' Brian closed his locker and left.

'Bye, Bri.'

Sabiha shook her head. 'I mean the way Jasper loves her and waits for her, even when she's being a bitch, that's true love.'

'Do you think so?' I leaned my arm on the locker next to her head.

'Yeah, every girl wants that.'

'What if some of them are like Saphire and don't see what's right in front of their nose?' I looked at her snub nose as I spoke, then my eyes drifted to her lips.

'No one would be that dumb. If there was such a guy, she'd get right on that.' Sabiha was oblivious.

'Would you?' I asked, waiting for her to make eye contact, and when she did, I leaned down. She blinked rapidly. This was it. This was my shot. I had to do it before I talked myself out of it. I moved in, aiming my lips for hers. She flinched, moving her head away.

I pushed myself off the locker, clenching my fists, as another sting of rejection burnt through me. 'I gotta go.' I slammed my locker shut. Why did I keep doing this to myself?

I walked away rapidly, not looking back at her. I heard her calling me but didn't turn back.

***

When I got home, Sarah had left bags of clothes in my bedroom with a congratulations card. She'd bought me another two pairs of jeans and seven t-shirts. I tried them on, liking what I saw. I'd spent most of my life attempting to be invisible and using my clothes as a shield. Today was the first time I'd realised that clothes weren't just about dressing for other people, it was about dressing for yourself. Instead of shying away from interacting with my peers, I felt comfortable returning nods and smiles.

I sat at my desk when my notifications told me I'd received an email. I opened my email and saw a message from a local newspaper wanting to interview me and Charlie. They'd seen the newsletter write-up that my English teacher, Ms Partridge, wrote about our graphic novel publication.

I called Charlie and asked him to check his email. I heard an intake of breath on the other line.

'Are you up for it?' I asked.

'Yes.'

'Okay, I'll reply.'

I was doubly relieved I had a new wardrobe. When Sarah came home, I was serving dinner. I approached her and hugged her tight, kissing her on the cheek. 'You like your new wardrobe.'

I nodded, smiling.

'Thank Brian too. He was my personal shopper and helped me pick it all out.'

We had dinner, and Mum and Sarah were so excited about my upcoming media opportunity. It wasn't until the next morning Brian came over again and helped me with my outfit, that the nerves hit. The journalist was keen to get us in the next issue and was coming to school today. As Brian blowdried my hair, I bit my lip nervously.

'Do you think it's too much?' I examined myself in the mirror.

My hair gleamed as he styled it in the Elvis cut, my medium-length hair with slightly trimmed sides and a tapered back. I looked like a new version of myself.

'Am I making a mistake being in the newspaper?' I'd been so excited the night before, I hadn't thought through about how it would make me the centre of attention. Was this a good thing?

'How could it be a mistake? The whole point is to publicise your book.' Brian squinted at my hair as he sprayed it with hairspray. 'Anyway, this is a good beginning to get used to your new life.'

When we arrived at the school, Brian ran to the girls ahead of me. 'A photographer and journalist are coming to the school today to interview Jesse and Charlie.'

Sabiha hadn't spoken since our near kiss the day before. I was still sore, but the butterflies about the newspaper were taking primary attention.

'Really!' Sabiha slapped my arm. 'Awesome. Everyone is going to know who you are.'

I nodded, forcing a smile. That's what I was worried about.

'You look worried? Why?' Sabiha looked at me with concern.

'I haven't exactly been the most popular kid at the school. I'm just wondering if this will leave another opening for people to attack me.'

'No, that won't happen.'

I tried to believe her.

'Listen, can we talk alone later?' Sabiha stepped in beside me as we walked to class.

I was distracted and unable to focus. 'Sure, sure,' I nodded.

At the beginning of PE, I handed Mr Robinson my note, excusing me from class.

'You going to the catwalk,' one of my classmates wolf-whistled, looking at my jeans and t-shirt.

'For your information, Jesse is having the local newspaper come and interview him.' Mr Robinson put his hand around my shoulders. 'Jesse is having a book published.'

'Whoopie.' They booed and threw the ball around.

'Ignore them, Jesse. I'm proud of you.' Mr Robinson said.

I nodded, feeling dejected as I walked out of the gym. I don't know why I thought things would be different. I was still the same person, and this wouldn't change anything. I entered the general office and found Charlie sitting in the chair across from reception. He was wearing his usual grey tracksuit pants and a grey t-shirt. Charlie's hair was trimmed and brushed back nicely. His mother had won that battle, at least.

I felt suddenly self-conscious in my new threads. I was trying too hard while Charlie was still himself. I cursed my ego, Sarah and Brian.

The journalist was due at 1.30 pm and then the photographer at 2.00. At 1.35, Charlie stirred, looked at the clock, and then back at me accusingly.

'She's probably just finding her way here.'

Charlie didn't reply, just continued staring at the clock.

At 1.37, a woman with blonde hair, the ends tipped pink, entered, looking flustered. She walked over to the reception. 'I'm Effie Giannopoulos, and I'm here to interview Jesse James and Charlie Lacertosa.'

After she signed in, the receptionist gestured to us. Effie approached, introducing herself and holding out her hand. I shook hands with her while Charlie kept his hands behind his back.

'You're seven minutes late,' Charlie said.

Effie's smile faded. 'Sorry about that. I had to park down the street.'

'Let's go sit in the conference room.' I gestured to the partitions to my left, leading to a conference room that Ms Partridge had arranged for us to use for the interview.

Charlie walked in and sat at the head of the table. I sat to his left and gestured for Effie to sit across from us.

'So, Charlie and Jesse, could you tell me about your graphic novel?'

I gave her the elevator pitch that I could now recite effortlessly.

'That sounds exciting. And what was the inspiration for the book?'

'Well, Jesse is in lo—'

I cut Charlie off. 'We wanted to combine various genres, romance, horror and humour. It was a bit of a challenge.' I'd told Charle not to share our inspiration of my feelings for Sabiha.

'But why? It's the truth.' Charlie was literal with no ability to disassemble.

'Yes, it is, but I don't want her to know that yet. It's something I'll tell her later,' I lied. I had decided I'd never tell Sabiha. She'd made her feelings more than clear for me. I needed to focus on the good thing coming from this—achieving my dream of becoming a writer.

Charlie looked at me but didn't continue.

'So you're both sixteen. You would have needed your parents to sign the contract,' Effie said.

'Yes, they didn't have the Superman clause.'

'What is that?'

Charlie explained the clause and added, 'And the $6,000 is being split into two payments.'

'You're getting paid $3,000 each?' Effie asked, looking at us with fresh eyes. 'How does it feel to be sixteen and getting paid that much?'

'Actually, that's the industry standard in Australia. We're hoping to publish it in the US and get another advance,' Charlie said.

'Another advance.' Effie was looking at us with awe.

She asked a few more questions about how long it took to write and our process. I heard the conversation at reception, and another woman peered. 'I'm Jackie, the photographer.' She had a camera around her neck.

'We'll just be a moment,' Effie said.

We finished the interview, and Effie spoke with Jackie, instructing her where to take photos.

Effie led us to the library, and we posed next to the bookshelves and desk. I felt quite ridiculous and selfconscious, as if everyone was staring at us. Charlie was blank-faced.

'Let's try a smile, Charlie,' Effie encouraged.

Charlie gave her the same expression. She and Jackie exchanged a look.

'Okay, maybe we'll try a serious author pose. The two of you just look this way.' Jackie pointed toward the windows while we stood sideways between the stacks.

Jackie held the camera up, and she and Effie examined the images through the preview, their faces troubled.

'Why don't Charlie and I work on our revisions while you take photos,' I suggested, knowing that Charlie could not relax for a photograph.

They nodded. We set up at our usual table. Charlie took out his sketchpad while I opened my laptop and found the version from our editor with suggested edits. Charlie began re-drawing the image while I tweaked the text. Jackie was still taking photos, but she was on the periphery of our vision as I lost myself in the writing process. I heard Jackie say they got what they needed. I stood and shook their hands, thanking them, relieved it was over.

Charlie and I stayed in the library working through lunch. Now that the newspaper article was over, I was brooding over Sabiha again and was looking to avoid her.

As Brian and I walked home, he was uncharacteristically subdued. 'You okay?'

He shrugged. 'Do you think people can tell?'

'Tell what?'

'That I'm gay.' He turned to me, his brown eyes full of pain.

'No, people can't tell. What happened?'

'Nothing, just the usual. People being assholes.'

'Why don't you come over, and we can play video games?'

He shook his head. 'No, I don't want to bring down your mood.'

I watched his lumbering walk to his house, feeling uneasy. I'd heard the sniggers and whispers, but they'd gotten louder since Brian came out. It was like our peers could feel his vulnerability and were striking.

**

A few days later, Sarah entered my bedroom, shrieking my name. I sat up with a jerk, looking around fearfully. 'It's here.' She opened the curtains and sat on the bed, holding up the newspaper.

I rubbed my eyes blearily and peered down. Charlie and I were sitting at our table. Charlie bent over his sketchbook, his face looking relaxed and almost content, while I looked at my laptop intently. We actually looked kind of okay.

'You look spunky,' Sarah said. 'Your shoulders look so broad.'

I smiled and read the article. The headline screamed "*Write of passage*," and the article gave our story of writing the book after school and included the advance amount.

I skimmed the article, caught by the closing paragraph. 'These two teens will use this advance to finance further equipment for future projects. This reporter believes they will score many more headlines soon.'

There was something so amazing when a stranger believed in your potential. I felt like I was walking on air as I got ready for school.

I walked with a spring in my step, wearing my new whitewashed jeans and a black t-shirt, Brian next to me.

As we entered the school grounds, a group of boys I did PE with walked past. 'Hello Jesse,' they nodded as they passed.

My knee nearly buckled. They were publicly saying hello to me after spending years bullying me. What was the world coming to?

'Hello to you too,' Brian shouted at them, angry that they'd snubbed him. 'Rude bastards.'

I sat on the bench next to Dina, purposely ignoring the space beside Sabiha. As we chatted, students passed, calling out my name and greeting me. I knew some of them as students I'd shared a class or two with over the years who had ignored me. And there were some that I was firmly convinced didn't know me at all but now saw me as someone they wanted to know.

Serena came over. 'Wow, I read the article about you and Charlie. Congratulations?' She pushed her long brown hair over her shoulder and smiled at me, her brown eyes sparkling under her thick eyelashes. 'I can't believe you're being paid $3,000. That's amazing.'

I gulped. Serena and I were in Food Technology together. We'd teamed up once in a while when her friend wasn't there, but she'd never deigned to talk to me outside of class.

'Yeah. The money's great. I'm just excited that I will be a published author and have people read my book.' I side-eyed Sabiha when I said it.

Serena's friend arrived. 'I have to go. See you in Food Tech.'

The bell went, and we drifted towards the lockers. Sabiha stepped in beside me. 'Listen, we haven't talked.'

'What about?' I didn't look at her as I kept walking.

'About the other day.'

'There's nothing to talk about.' I cut her off. 'Message received.'

I didn't wait for her to respond, walking away from her. There was something to be said about having the last word. It sure tasted sweet.

Chapter 17

I walked to school and joined Dina and Sabiha on the bench. I thought Brian was already at school. He hadn't been waiting at my house, so I knocked at his door, but there was no answer.

'Hey Jesse,' Sabiha greeted me.

I nodded at her, saying nothing.

Ten minutes passed, and Alma hadn't arrived. She was usually so punctual. 'Is everything okay with Alma? She's usually here by now.'

'How should I know?' Sabiha snapped.

I gave her a cold look before turning back to Dina. 'Why don't you check on her?'

'Yeah, you're right. She's usually here by now.' Dina's face creased with concern, and she took out her phone.

'Sorry I snapped,' Sabiha bit her lip as she looked at me. 'It's just a sore spot.'

'Well, as long as it's all about you,' I drawled, not looking at her.

Sabiha gasped. Usually I was never this cruel, always choosing kindness and the high road, but now a switch had been flipped. I was sick of tiptoeing around her and would no longer bite back my words.

'Aren't you the little firecracker today?' Dina gripped my shoulders, giving me a warning look. 'You'd think your success has gone to your head.'

'Maybe it has. Maybe I won't let anyone treat me like shit anymore.' I turned to Sabiha.

Her eyes widened, and she bit her lip. 'But I didn't — I don't' She didn't finish the sentence.

Now that I saw that I'd scored a point, guilt hit me. She looked so helpless.

'Sorry. I haven't had breakfast today,' I said weakly, offering a weak excuse.

'Oh.' Sabiha's face cleared, and she looked like she was trying to decide whether or not to believe me.

'I got you.' Dina opened her backpack and took out a muesli bar.

'Thanks.' I opened it and chewed, needing to make the lie a truth.

Dina took out her mobile and dialled for Alma. 'Where are you?' she asked.

There was a pause as Alma answered.

'Come to the front,' Dina demanded.

A pause again.

'Why is there an echo?' Dina asked. 'Are you in the toilets? Do you need a tampon?'

Dina moved the phone away from her ear and asked Sabiha if she had a tampon.

'Yeah,' Sabiha nodded.

'Which toilets are you in?' Dina asked. 'She's in the three-storey building.'

Sabiha walked ahead, and Dina stepped in with me. 'What's going on with you?' she asked. 'You've never been like that with Sabiha.'

'I've had enough. I keep trying, and she's just always rejecting me.'

'What did you try?' she asked.

'The other day, at the lockers. I tried to kiss her, and she flinched.'

'Oh, that. That's not about you. That's about her.' She waved her hand.

'What are you talking about?' I demanded.

'You know, her whole thing with men.' Her face creased with confusion.

I stopped walking and tugged her arm, making her stop too. 'What thing?' I asked.

'She should tell you. It's not my place.' Dina held his hands up and walked away.

I brooded, watching Sabiha's back as she walked ahead of me. What was Dina talking about? It seemed she believed there was a reason Sabiha backed off, and it wasn't because she was rejecting me. I'd been convinced that she would have another 'just friends' talk I hadn't given her the time of day. Was I wrong to blow her off?

We reached the toilets, and Sabiha waited for Dina to catch up, carefully avoiding my gaze. I waited a bit, then realised I looked creepy loitering outside the girls' toilets. I returned to my locker, exchanged my backpack for my books for the first two sessions, and went to the front to wait for Brian.

A few minutes later, the girls came, Alma in tow wearing Dina's jumper, a school uniform dress peeking from below its hem. Mmm, she must have put on her old school uniform to school and now was embarrassed.

'Where's Brian?' Sabiha asked when she joined me.

'He didn't come to the door when I knocked,' I said. 'I thought he was already here.'

Dina and Sabiha shook their heads.

'I'll call him.' I took out my mobile. 'Hey Bri, where are you?' I listened to his response but couldn't understand what he was saying. 'What do you mean?' He pulled the phone away from his ear. 'He told me to jump in my bunker because he's going nuclear.'

'What does that mean?' Sabiha demanded. 'Give me the phone. I'll call him.'

'No need,' Alma said, catching sight of Brian's approach.

We followed her gaze. Brian wore skin-tight leather pants, a mesh see-through top, and chunky bikie boots, with foundation on his face. His skin was shiny and blemish-free, and his lips were a matte colour. He had outlined his eyes with eyeliner, dark eye shadow and mascara, making them look like topaz jewels.

Oh, shit. Brian had now gone and done it. He'd completely outed himself. What was going to happen to him? My heart broke because I knew what his father was like, but something in the way he walked, looking so confident and happy because he was completely himself, filled me with pride. I could see how much joy it brought him to not have to hide anymore.

The group next to us laughed. 'Where's the homo brigade?' one girl said loudly enough for Brian to hear as he drew alongside them.

Brian stopped and gave the girl a once-over. 'I can dress straight, but you can never change ugly.'

The girl gasped, and everyone else laughed. Things settled, and they all returned their eyes to their respective groups. The moment for ugliness had passed, for now.

'Hello beautiful people,' Brian said cheerily.

'What brought this on?' I gestured at his outfit.

'I figured if people were going to call me a faggot, I might as well live up to their expectations,' he said with a smile full of bravado.

I still couldn't believe Adnan had called him that, but even with that, I still felt a pang of sympathy.

'You look like a gay cliché,' Sabiha said.

'This is what they expect, isn't it?' Brian said.

Sabiha rolled her eyes. 'It doesn't mean you have to lower yourself to their expectations.'

They had a staring contest until Dina stepped in and slapped Brian's shoulder. 'I hope you brought a change of clothes. If you go home like that, your dad will go nuts.'

'That's not a problem,' Brian said flatly.

'Of course it is,' Dina insisted. 'Your Dad is always on your back about you being not blokey enough. If he saw you in makeup, he'd blow a gasket.'

'Don't be a spoilsport,' Sabiha said.

'Shut up,' Dina snapped. 'Not everyone has a mum like yours who doesn't get on your back about everything. The rest of us have parents whose love has boundaries and if we cross them, we're out. No second chances.' She turned back to Brian. 'Do you have a change of clothes?'

'No,' Brian said.

'For fuck's sake, Brian—'

'He said it won't be a problem—' Sabiha interrupted.

'Because my dad already saw me,' Brian continued in a regular conversational tone.

Dina and Sabiha were struck dumb. I listened with fisted hands as he told us about his father catching him wearing makeup in his mother's room and how he'd kicked him out. I always knew his father was a tough bastard, but I hadn't realised he was heartless too. Dina and Sabiha attempted to comfort him, but he quickly rebuffed them, pretending this wasn't a body blow.

'What are you going to do now?' Dina asked, on the verge of hysteria. 'Where are you going to live?'

Brian looked dazed as if he'd only realised he was homeless.

'He'll be fine.' I put a calming hand on Dina's shoulders. 'He'll stay at my house.'

Dina took a deep, gulping breath.

Brian's face cleared. 'Thanks. I'll talk to my brother Greg tomorrow and sort something out.'

I nodded. 'However long you need.'

There was a pause as everyone processed. Brian gazed at Alma. 'What do you think, Alma?'

'I think you're very brave,' she said. 'Coming out at high school isn't easy, but lying about who you are isn't either.'

'Let's hope he did it for the right reason,' I added archly. I knew this was his revenge against Adnan. He was striking back once and for all against Adnan.

'What have we here?' Brian demanded as he saw Alma tug Dina's jumper down, trying to cover her uniform. 'Is this a fashion *faux pas*?'

I watched Brian drag Alma to the girl's bathroom, singing the Ghost Busters theme song and talking about a masterpiece.

I followed and stopped short at the female toilets. Not again. I was going to be a class creep if I kept doing this. Two girls scuttled out, giving me a wide-eyed look. Shit, Brian was going to get into a world of trouble being in the girl's toilets. Sabiha and Dina burst through the doors after them. Sabiha followed the girls while Dina stood in front of the door.

'What's he doing in there?' I asked.

'Giving Alma a makeover.'

'Get him to leave.' If Brian was caught, he'd be suspended the same day he was kicked out of home.

'Sure, I'll do that. And while I'm at it I'll end world hunger and bring about world peace,' Sabiha drawled.

I gave her a dirty look.

'Make yourself useful.' She tugged me to her side and made me face the hallway. 'Look intimidating and scare anyone coming in.'

Sabiha returned.

'Did you neutralise the girls?' Dina asked.

Sabiha popped her knuckles. 'They won't be talking, or they'll be sleeping with the fishes.'

My eyes widened. 'Did you threaten them?'

Sabiha laughed. 'No, nothing so drastic. Just told them Brian was having a hard time. They agreed not to dob him into the teacher.'

Sabiha joined Dina to stand guard in front of the toilets while I moved to the window, out of earshot. A little while later, Alma stepped out, and my breath caught in my throat.

Brian had somehow made the uniform fitted and outlined her eyes so they were doe-like while her lips were shiny and plump.

'What do you think, Jesse?' Brian asked. 'You like?'

My eyes went up and down, and I felt slightly dazed. 'You look amazing.' This was truly the moment when I could see the resemblance between the sisters. She reminded me so much of Sabiha on the night of the superhero party, and my pulse raced as I tripped down memory lane, remembering my first kiss with Sabiha.

Sabiha frowned. 'She looks okay.'

'This is my masterpiece you're talking about.' Brian was indignant.

'She's young for that get up,' Sabiha said.

'You remember your Wonder Woman costume for my comic book party?' Brian asked archly.

'Yes, I remember,' Sabiha snapped. 'You were the one who hired it, and I was the one who got burnt by it.'

They both looked embarrassed. Were they talking about my kiss with Sabiha, or her kiss with Brian? I felt a pang as I remembered the rest of that night and that Sabiha had gone straight from my arms to Brian's.

Brian looked away first. 'Maybe she is young.' He yanked Alma to the side of the hallway and rearranged her clothes. 'There. Do we get the big sister stamp of approval?'

Sabiha nodded. 'Much better.'

At lunchtime, I ducked into the library to work with Charlie, for once regretting that I'd arranged the day before. I wanted to speak to Sabiha but was scared too. Dina ran in, wild-eyed and panting. 'There was a fight at the canteen. Sabiha and Brian were involved.'

My stomach dropped. 'Is Sabiha okay?'

Dina nodded, gulping deep breaths. 'She's okay. But Brian is getting suspended.'

I ran with her to the sub school where Brian was sitting in front of the coordinator, Ms Hastings. She was staring at the phone in consternation while Brian stared blankly at the wall behind her. 'Your father is refusing to come to school. He said you're not to come home today. What's going on?'

'He's a homophobe.' Brian crossed his legs and sat up straight. 'I'm better off without him.'

'Brian's staying at my house,' I interrupted, while Dina panted quietly beside me.

Ms Hastings looked at me gratefully. 'Good, good. Looks like your father needs some time to process.' She frowned again. 'We still need an adult to confirm.'

'You can call my sister Sarah.' I'd messaged Sarah after Brian's coming out and told her he was staying over. I wrote the number for Ms Hastings on her notepad and slid it to her.

'Are you okay?' I asked as I sat in the chair next to him. Dina stood behind him, her hands on his shoulders.

'Peachy,' he muttered, looking anything but.

Ms Hastings hung up. 'Alright, that's settled. Sarah said you can stay with them while your dad calms down.'

Brian snorted. He knew his father would not calm down anytime soon.

'For now, you can stay in the school office until the end of the day.' She pointed to the office behind them.

Brian nodded and stood, twirling on his heel and sashaying to the back while Dina and I walked out together.

'He'll be fine. I'll take care of him.'

Dina nodded, tears glistening in her eyes.

'I didn't realise you and Brian were so close?' I'd never seen her so emotional.

She shredded a tissue in her hands. 'My brother got kicked out by my parents, and he dropped off the radar. I don't want the same thing happening to Brian.'

'It won't.' I rubbed her arm.

'Thanks Jesse.'

At the end of the day, we met at the lockers and walked home. I'd seen Sabiha in passing between class. She looked none the worse for wear, and Dina had updated her about Brian's new status.

When we got to my house, garbage bags were on the front porch. I frowned. Who had left rubbish there? I opened one bag and peered in, pulling out a blue velvet shirt I recognised as Brian's.

'Daddy dearest is wasting no time in cleaning the house.' Brian shoved the shirt back in the bag, his cheeks turning pink.

I helped him carry the bags into the house and into my room.

'I'm going to go for a job,' Brian said. He rifled through the bags, pulled out a t-shirt and shorts, and left the house.

I knew he just needed time and prepared dinner while he was gone. While we were eating a subdued dinner, his brother Greg came, and I heard raised voices from the porch. When I asked Brian what happened, he didn't want to talk about it.

The next few days, we settled into a rhythm of being uneasy roommates. I was quietly relieved when he announced he was moving in with Dina's brother. My room was not big enough for an ongoing roommate.

Chapter 18

As I walked into the house Omer and Brian were sharing, I saw the housewarming party was in full swing. The living room was full of sketchy guys. The crowd moved slightly, and I saw Sabiha smiling at a guy doing the Michael Jackson moonwalk. I wanted to turn around and walk out when Sabiha looked at me and waved.

Don't assume the worst, James, I attempted to calm the adrenaline coursing through me.

'I didn't think we'd see you here,' I said to Alma after I'd greeted each Sabiha. 'Sabiha said you weren't coming.'

'Sabiha doesn't speak for me,' Alma snapped, and the tension between the sisters filled the air.

'Hello my peeps.' Brian stumbled into us, breaking the tense silence. He hugged me and Sabiha, then ended up leaning against them. 'Are you enjoying my little soiree? That's right, it's not a little soiree. It's a fucking frat party.' He spat out as he looked around.

The party mood had changed.

'Maybe we should leave.' I looked at the guys shouting and egging each other on into drinking games, and the few girls in attendance were leaving.

'No, please don't go,' Brian urged. 'Let's have our own party.' He collected booze. 'We'll hide in my room. It will be like Switzerland.'

We followed his lead, collected snacks, plates and drinks, and followed him down the hall. We piled into Brian's bedroom and put all our goodies on his student desk.

'Let's make sure we don't have any interruptions.' Brian lifted his chest of drawers, and I helped place them against the door. The doorknob rattled. There was a bang on the door, and the interloper moved on.

Brian turned on his lamp, making the room more intimate. He hit a few buttons on his computer, and music began playing. 'I prepared my own party mix. But the powers that be told me it was too gay for them. Who wants a hit?' Brian did an imitation of a bartender in a loud club who couldn't hear the drink's orders.

I sat on the bed next to Alma. 'How have you been settling into the new school?' In my quest to avoid Sabiha, I'd avoided Alma too and hadn't had the chance to check in with her.

'It's been really great,' Alma said.

'Have seen little of you lately.' Sabiha sat next to me and interjected herself into the conversation.

'I've been busy,' I said, stretching the truth. 'I'm revising my graphic novel.' We both knew I'd been avoiding her. I'd only spoken to her to check in after her locker was vandalised a few days before, otherwise, I'd spent my lunchtimes with Charlie.

Sabiha nodded awkwardly and took a sip of her drink. 'Are you making a lot of changes?'

'Just smoothing out the structure so it reads better.'

'If you ever need another pair of eyes...' Sabiha said.

'I thought you didn't like graphic novels?' Alma said.

'This is different,' Sabiha fumbled, and her cheeks flushed. 'This is Jesse's comic book, and I want to help in any way I can.'

I was taken aback to see her confident veneer dented. Did she care what I thought?

'Who's your publisher?' Alma asked.

'Gordonio,' I replied, still pondering Sabiha's strange reaction.

'They published the Mikado Chronicles.'

I turned to Alma, surprised to find that she was a fan of graphic novels, and we chatted about our favourites.

Sabiha shifted on the bed and nudged me. 'So you and Serena have been spending some time together?'

I frowned. 'Not really. She just wanted to see how the graphic novel was shaping up.' Brian and I had been working in the computer room in the library at lunchtime when Serena stepped in to chat. I hadn't realised Sabiha was in the library too and had seen us. 'Why didn't you come over?'

'I was busy borrowing some books for the weekend.' Sabiha smiled tipsily, nudging closer to me.

'Okay.'

Sabiha and Alma went through the window to pee, as Brian refused to let them open the door.

The sisters returned, the tension between them again. Alma sat by herself, looking forlorn and worried.

'Are you okay?' I asked her.

She nodded.

'Did something happen while you were alone outside?' Was Sabha cruel to her again?

'No, of course not.'

I heard squealing and saw that Dina was turning green. Sabiha helped Dina lean out the window and held her hair back as she vomited, looking like she was fighting her gag reflex.

'I have to wait for my taxi.' Alma stood.

'I can't leave Dina and wait with you,' Sabiha said.

'I don't need you to,' Alma snapped.

Sabiha looked annoyed.

'I'll come with you,' I said, attempting to defuse the situation.

Sabiha looked uneasily between the two of us. 'She'll be fine. Anyway, I can see the street from here.'

'There's drunk idiots everywhere,' I snapped. Was she really going to risk her sister's safety like this?

I followed Alma out the window.

'So what's the deal between you and Sabiha?' Alma asked as we waited for the taxi at the front of the house.

I shifted uncomfortably. 'We're just friends.'

'Does she know that?'

I frowned in confusion.

'You get that she's totally into you, right?' Alma smiled crookedly.

'We had a thing for a moment, but she moved on.' Even though I was trying to, I still couldn't move on.

'I hate to burst your bubble, but she didn't move on,' Alma said wryly.

I looked at the house. Was it really true? The front door opened, and my pulse sped up as I hoped it was Sabiha. Instead, Brian shouted for me. I walked over.

'I need you to take over. I can't hold my gag reflex anymore.' Brian looked green around the gills. Unfortunately, I'd developed a much tougher constitution than him after being Mum's career during chemo. There had been many a chuck bucket and mop-ups.

'You have to be with Alma. She can't stay by herself outside.' I pointed to Alma standing on the curve by herself.

'You got it.' Brian moved aside and closed the door after I entered.

I called out to Alma about what was going on and went down the hallway. The bathroom door was closed, and I knocked. Sabiha opened it, looking frazzled.

'Brian sent me.'

She nodded and stepped away from the door. 'She's like the poltergeist.'

Dina was bent over the toilet, heaving, and heavy splashes hit the water in the toilet. She gasped as she lifted her head. 'That's it. Nothing's left.' Tears were streaming down her face, and her cheeks were flushed.

'Good, because that was quite a performance.' Just as Dina's mouth opened, Sabiha stepped forward and another splash of vomit came hurling out, all over Sabiha's runners.

Sabiha looked down in horror, her face working through emotion. 'Fuck, fuck, fuck.'

Dina wiped her mouth. 'Now, there's definitely nothing left.'

I stifled a smile and washed out a glass, filling it with water and handing it to Dina.

Sabiha toed off her runners, her mouth puckered in disgust and went to stand in the bathtub. There was a mop in the recess next to the washing machine. I wet it and mopped up the vomit off the tiled floor. I put the mop in the laundry sink. 'I'll find you some shoes from Brian.'

Sabiha nodded gratefully.

I went to Brian's room and rifled through his wardrobe, finding a pair of runners I took back to Sabiha.

The music cut out, and a scream cut through the air.

'Shit. This is turning out to be some shit show.' I left them in the bathroom and walked toward the living room, seeing partygoers running from the house.

A guy in a red singlet was standing threateningly over Omer. 'You've been hard to find, amigo.'

Another goon with a bald head shoved Alex up against the wall while a third pushed me and Brian on the couch and grabbed Omer's arm, holding him in place.

'I've been here the whole time, Louie.' Omer winced in pain as the goon holding him squeezed his arm.

'I thought maybe you forgot about me, and you know that wouldn't be good for your health.' Louie's attention wandered as Dina stumbled in, weaving drunkenly as she dodged furniture.

Dina grabbed Omer's arm to keep herself upright, moving him away from Louie's mate.

'So that's what's been keeping you busy, brother?' He smiled approvingly as he looked Dina up and down. 'And what's your name?'

Dina answered, wearing a lop-sided smile.

Omer looked sick as he watched Dina flirting with Louie. Realising that Omer was too scared to do anything, I stood and reached for Dina, wanting to get her away from Louis.

The bald goon pushed me back onto the sofa.

My fists clenched, and I went to stand again, but Brian grabbed my arm. 'Don't. Let's just wait for them to leave.'

I subsided, not wanting to make the situation worse.

'It's a shame Omer got to you first.' Louie gave Omer a sly smile.

'I'm not his girlfriend,' Dina said.

Omer approached them. 'About our business—'

'I'm his sister,' Dina said before Omer reached her.

It was like watching a car accident in slow motion. 'You're Omer's sister. Did you hear that, boys?' Louie asked the two guys that were with him. They took that as their cue and surrounded Omer, each grabbing an arm. 'If your sister and I go for a drive, I'll give you an extra three days to pay your loan.'

The goons had moved away from me and Brian and held Omer, who was struggling. Brian looked at me helplessly. I had to do something, but what?

Louis took Dina in his arms. She looked completely unaware of what was going on. Sabiha burst into the living room wearing Brian's jeans and a top. 'Dina, you owe me a new pair of shoes.' Her gaze sharpened when she saw Louie and his mates. 'What's going on here?'

I sidled closer to Dina and Louis, determined to snatch her from his arms.

'We're settling a debt owed by Omer,' Louie said.

Dina leaned limply against him. She looked like she'd fall down but he held her up effortlessly, his biceps bunching up. He carelessly ran his hands through her hair, petting her like a dog. Dina leaned against Louie's shoulder, drunkenly smiling, oblivious to the danger.

'How much?' Sabiha demanded.

'Get ready,' Omer whispered in my ear as Sabiha and Louis talked.

My gaze sharpened, and I waited, my fists clenched.

Louis began molesting Dina, and she struggled. Omer threw himself forward and aimed a punch at Louie's face. Louie dodged his punch and dropped Dina, who landed on the floor with a thud. The goon grabbed Omer and held him while Louie punched him in the torso.

Sabiha ran forward and pulled Dina toward the front door. Dina screamed and tried to return to her brother, but Sabiha relentlessly yanked her away. I grabbed Dina's other arm, and we ran.

'The back door,' Sabiha shouted.

As we burst through the door and into the backyard, Alma joined us from the driveway, her eyes wide-eyed with panic.

Sabiha reached the back fence. 'Jump over.' Sabiha lifted Dina's leg and put it on the beam. 'Hurry. We have to get help for Omer.'

Dina finally cooperated. Brian lithely jumped over while I perched on top of the fence and helped Dina over first, glad I had the upper body strength to heave her over while Sabiha pushed. I helped Alma and Sabiha over, before jumping down from the fence into someone else's backyard. We ran down the side of the house.

'Who's got a phone?' Sabiha demanded when we hit the footpath.

'Me.' Alma rifled through my handbag and looked up in panic. 'I dropped it.'

'What are we going to do?' Dina sounded like a wounded animal.

'I'm thinking.' Sabiha looked up and down the street.

'I'll run to my house,' I said. 'It will only take 10 minutes.'

'Too long.' Sabiha's gaze zeroed in on a house across the street. 'I'll ask to use their phone.'

'You can't go alone.' I grabbed her arm.

Sabiha waited.

'Let's go.' I followed her to the house and knocked on the door. An elderly woman answered, leaning on a walking stick. 'Hello, we need some help. A friend just had a birthday party, and there were some gatecrashers. We need to call the police.'

The woman peered out at the Sassy Saints behind us. Seeing Dina sobbing on the footpath while Brian comforted her, her face creased with concern. 'Of course. Of course.'

I held my hand up, allowing Sabiha to go first. She dialled triple zero and told the police the same story, adding the address. I was so relieved she was okay. There were a million ways the party could have gone wrong.

After we called the police, we walked back to the house, Dina and Sabiha having a biffo about her brother while the rest of us pretended we didn't hear. When we reached the house, Dina tried to tear ahead, but Sabiha carelessly grabbed her into a bear hug and covered her mouth when she protested.

'I think they're gone.' I peered through the darkness to see if Louie's car was gone.

'We should wait until the police arrive,' Sabiha said.

Dina violently protested, shaking her head as she tried to shake off Sabiha's bear hold.

I met Dina's panicked gaze and couldn't let her suffer anymore. She was in agony worrying about her brother. 'I'll see if it's all clear. You all wait here.'

'I'm coming.' Brian ran a few paces and joined me.

'This is bullshit,' Sabiha said with disgust, letting go of Dina. 'We're not waiting like some pathetic Victorian maidens that need to be saved.'

I turned, ready to argue with Sabiha. This was one time when her fearless attitude was a liability, and I was determined to keep her safe.

A police car drove past. 'They're here.' Dina ran.

In the living room, Omer was on the couch, his face bruised and his eyeball red. 'They were Asian,' he told the police officers, giving a wrong description. 'They crashed the party and lay into me.'

I opened my mouth to correct him, but Omer shook his head quickly. I quietened down as the police officer asked us questions.

'Why did you lie?' Sabiha asked when the police left.

'Louie told me he'd cut up Dina if I went to the cops.' Omer had his arm around Dina. They argued about Louis going to the hospital, but he refused. He didn't want too many questions asked. Brian and I carried him to the bathroom, where we tended to his cuts and bandaged him up, before helping him to his bedroom and into bed. I left Brian to make him more comfortable and returned to the living room. Sabiha was cleaning up while Dina sat on the couch, her eyes droopily closed.

'Where's Alma?' I peered into the empty kitchen.

'She's gone home.' Sabiha was holding a rubbish bin and throwing in plastic cups and beer bottles.

My skin rose in goose-pimples. 'How is she getting home?'

'Alex drove her.'

'You let her go with that sleaze bag.' My voice came out louder than I intended. I sprinted out the front door and peered down the street, but they were gone.

Sabiha followed, looking at me in confusion. 'She'll be fine.'

'What the hell is wrong with you?' I demanded. 'You know what he's like, and you're acting like it's no big deal that she's alone in a car with Alex Payne, Mr Blowjob Lane himself.'

'You know, she's my sister—

'Exactly,' I cut her off. 'She's your sister, and yet you're caring for her less than I would for a dog on the street.'

Sabiha gasped, looking at me wide-eyed.

All my rage built up, and I couldn't hold it back as it spilled over. 'I know you're hurt or whatever because of your father, but this selfish, self-centred attitude is a really bad look.' I brushed past her and back into the house. 'Have you got Alma's phone number?' I asked Dina as Sabiha followed me and stood in the doorway.

Dina blinked at me sleepily and took her phone from her pocket. 'Yes.'

'Good. Can you message Alma and make sure she got home okay?'

Dina looked at me in confusion.

'Alex Payne was dropping her off,' I added.

Dina's confusion cleared as her eyes widened with concern. 'Shit.' She tapped on her phone.

I refused to look at Sabiha, even though I could see that she was now hunched in concern.

'She's okay,' Dina breathed a sigh of relief as she read Alma's message.

'No thanks to her so-called big sister,' I snapped. It wasn't like me to keep haranguing an argument, but I couldn't shore it back up now that the dam was opened.

'Wow,' I heard Brian behind me. 'What am I missing?'

'Nothing much.' Sabiha straightened. 'It seems Jesse has got the hots for my sister.'

'Are you serious?' I turned toward her, my cheeks flushed with rage. 'Just because I'm acting like I give a shit, I must have the hots for her?'

'The two of you disappeared together, and Alma came back with her buttons askew.' Sabiha crossed her arms and glared at me.

Suddenly, my rage muted, and my voice became dangerously calm. 'Do you really believe that?'

Sabiha stilled, her bluster fading.

'That's a yes or a no question. Do you believe I would be that sort of guy?'

Sabiha mutely shook her head.

'So then, why would you say that?' I demanded.

'You care so much about Alma, I thought maybe you were into her.' Sabiha averted her gaze and looked uncomfortable.

'Why would you— What the— Ahhh,' I shouted in exasperation. 'I am so sick of this.'

'Okay, let's have a time out.' Brian tugged me to the backdoor.

I resisted, my blood burning with rage and all the unspoken words I wanted to say. Seeing Sabiha's shock, my rage muted. 'Fine.' I snapped and followed him outside. I paced in the backyard while he watched.

'Do you want to tell me what's going on?' Brian asked gently.

'She treats me like a toy,' I ground out between gritted teeth.

'Okay.' Brian nodded.

I paced until the anger burnt itself out and then sat on the plastic chair under the hills hoist, leaning back to stare at the full moon on the horizon.

'There's someone here to talk to you,' Brian called out.

I turned and saw Sabiha next to him. I turned back to the moon, saying nothing. She got another chair and dragged it next to me.

'I'm sorry,' she said softly. 'I shouldn't have made such a terrible accusation about you and Alma.'

I grunted in affirmation but didn't turn to look at her.

'I guess I got jealous and thought you were developing feelings for her.'

I turned to her, caught by the word jealous. 'Why were you jealous?'

'Well, because...' she twisted her hands in her lap, looking down at her feet.

I'd never seen her looking so vulnerable.

She breathed in and met my gaze.

I almost allowed myself to believe that she had feelings for me, her gaze soft, her lips softly parted, as if she were inviting me for a kiss.

'Because what?' I asked again.

She flushed and looked down at her hands.

'I've put myself out there time and time again, and every time, you reject. Even the other day at the lockers, when I went to kiss you, you flinched.'

Her head lifted. 'That's not because of you.'

'Then why?' I asked.

She bit her lip, hesitating.

I stood, wanting to end the conversation.

'It happened when we lived with Mum's boyfriend, Dave.' Her small voice carried from the darkness. 'They had a party. During the party, Baz, Dave's mate, came to my bedroom while I was sleeping. He said that I'd egged him on with my flirting. I didn't think I was flirting. He was complimenting me, and was so much older, like a dad, and I was just saying stuff. He tried to, you know.' She sighed. 'Anyway, since then, I get kind of weird around guys.'

I turned to look at her. She looked embarrassed. 'I'm sorry. That guy was a jerk. I'd never do that to you.'

'I know that.' She stood and approached me. 'I know you're not like him. I just struggle when things go too fast.' She was now so close I felt her breath on my face. She turned up her face and met my gaze. Slowly, she stood on her tiptoes and pressed her lips to mine.

I wanted to put my arms around her but was too scared I'd scare her off, so I let my lips do the talking, kissing her back, trying to pour all my feelings into my kiss.

She broke the kiss, her eyes heavy-lidded and her lips swollen.

'Why now?' I asked. 'Why didn't you like me before?'

'I did.' Her eyes cleared. 'I always liked you. I was just too scared.'

I'd spent so long trying, wanting her to have the same feelings for me, and yet now, I couldn't believe it. 'Then why did you kiss Brian after we kissed?'

'I'm sorry, I was messed up. I didn't realise that the only reason I had feelings for Brian was because I felt safe with him.'

'But you knew I like you and that he was my best friend, and you still kissed him. Were you trying to hurt me?'

She bit her lip, looking torn. 'Maybe,' she said carefully. 'Maybe on some level I was trying to push you away. That's why I did all that stuff with Brian.'

My skin prickled as if someone had walked on my grave. 'Stuff?' I demanded. 'You and Brian did more than kiss?'

She stilled and nodded hesitantly. 'I thought you knew? After the graffiti on the locker.'

I shook my head. I'd known there were shitty things written and condoms put in her locker, but by the time I saw it, everything was wiped clean. Did everyone else know but me?

'Did you have sex?' I asked, my throat tight.

'We didn't have sex, but we did—'

'No,' I lifted my hand. 'I don't want to know.'

'I'm sorry,' she cried. 'I'm so sorry. I like you, I really do.'

I stood, my legs wobbling. 'I have to go.' I entered the house, and Brian appeared like a Jack in the Box.

'What happened?' Seeing my face, his smile faded, and he looked concerned.

'You and Sabiha, you did more than kiss?'

He stilled, looking like he was trying to decide whether or not to lie.

'She told me.'

He deflated. 'I'm sorry, Jesse. I never would have if I knew you liked her.'

I took a deep, shuddering breath. I wanted to be angry at him, I really did, but it was true. He didn't know.

I looked back at Sabiha outside, her soft sobs travelling on the night air. Was I being unfair? After all, this was history. I wanted to go out and talk to her, forgive her, but my feet wouldn't move.

'Go.' Brian pushed me gently toward the front door. 'I'll take care of her.'

I nodded and turned, and left. I needed a time-out to process what I was thinking and feeling.

Chapter 19

The next day was Sunday, and I was drinking tea in the kitchen, staring out the window, when Sarah walked in from the living room where she and Mum were watching TV. It was mid-morning, and I'd slept in, while they'd been up for hours.

'How was the party last night?' she asked, pouring herself a tea and sitting the kitchen table. She'd asked Mum if she wanted a cuppa, who'd said no.

'Good.' I lied. I didn't want to tell her about the gatecrashers.

'Are you sure? Because you don't look like it was good.'

'No, no. It was.'

She stared at me sceptically as she sipped her tea.

'Something happened.' I cleared my throat and sat. 'Sabiha and I kissed.'

Sarah's smile lit up, and her blue eyes danced. 'Really. So you're together?'

'No.' I rubbed my neck. 'I found out some stuff, and now I feel all mixed up.'

I told her about my conversation with Sabiha and her telling me about what happened to her when she was young and about her doing more than kissing Brian.

'Poor Sabiha. That sort of thing can be really traumatising. No wonder she struggles with romantic entanglements and keeps picking unavailable men.'

My gaze sharpened as I backtracked through Sabiha's crush history. Brian and Edo, both of them unsuitable for different reasons.

'That's what she said. I mean, she said that she liked Brian because he was safe, and she confused friendship with romance.'

'I can see that happening. There would be no romance vibes from Brian, while you....'

'Me what?' I demanded when she didn't finish.

'You've been really into her since day one. Women can pick up that sort of intensity, so that's probably why she struggled to be with you. On the one hand, she liked you. On the other hand, you liking her made her feel unsafe because of the sexual tension.'

I sat back in the chair, remembering all the times that Sabiha flinched when I attempted to kiss her, or approached her physically. All this time I thought it was all about me, but now I realised it was about her.

'This is good.' Sarah reached over and took my hand. 'Now the two of you have properly communicated, you've got a good foundation to make a real go of this relationship.'

I blinked as my eyes burnt 'I don't know if I can forgive her. She knew I liked her, and then she went and did stuff with Brian.'

'Well, that's up to you. You need to decide if you're going to move forward, or keep being hung up on the past.'

'I just wish...'

Sarah waited.

'I just wish I had some way of knowing that this was different. That she was different. We've had so many near misses and drama. Maybe I've been trying too hard to make something happen that shouldn't.'

'I don't know, Jesse. No one is perfect. All we can do is accept each other and move on.' Sarah patted my hand and went to the kitchen.

I went to my bedroom and lay in bed, holding my phone, debating whether to send a message to Sabiha. I didn't want her to think everything was okay because I wasn't sure it was. But I also wanted her to know that we were okay as friends.

I sent her a cat meme, two cats lying side by side with their paws entangled. 'Best friends forever.' I saw she read it and waited for a reply. There were three dots as she wrote a reply, and then her cat meme, a kitten hiding behind a door, 'I sorry.'

I sighed with relief. Okay, we were back to friendship. At least we were communicating.

***

Monday morning, Brian was waiting on the street for me. 'Are you okay?

'Yeah, all good.' I forced a smile.

He stepped in, and we walked to school together. 'What about you and Sabiha?'

I shrugged.

'Because I think the two of you belong together, and I feel so shit that I'm the reason—'

'You're not the reason. I am.' I'd had the afternoon to think about it all and realised what was holding me back. 'I don't know if I can trust her. I've spent so much time pining for her, waiting for her to notice me, and now,' I took a deep breath. 'Now I can't trust that it's real and she's really into me.'

'But you know Sabiha fakes nothing?'

'I know. But I also know she can be fickle and selfish, putting her own needs above everyone else.'

Brian bit his lip, not denying what I was saying. 'Are you willing to throw away a shot at love because you can't trust?'

'Maybe.' I moodily kicked a pebble as I walked. 'I'm just so sick of being hurt, Bri.'

Brian went to open his mouth but bit back his words. 'Okay.'

When we reached the school, Sabiha watched me, her lips parted, her eyes gleaming with anticipation.

'Hi.' I nodded.

Her face dropped in disappointment, but she said hello back.

'Let's talk.' I waved toward the bush, and we both walked over together. 'I just wanted to let you know that I'm not angry with you about what happened with Brian. It was a long time, and it's history.'

'Okay.' She pushed her hair off her smile and stepped closer, her hand on my chest.

I looked down and hesitated.

'I just don't know if we should try to be more than friends. I mean, it hasn't worked until now. Maybe we should just play it safe.'

'Oh.' She took her hand away, and I felt a chill where her hand had been. 'Okay, if that's what you want.'

I nodded, now that I'd actually said it, feeling anything but certain. *What the hell are you doing, James?,* a voice hissed in my head. *You finally had your shot, and now you're blowing it.*

We returned to the group, Dina and Brian watching us with concern.

'Hey Jesse.' Serena approached. 'Are you going to be at the library today?' She twirled her hair as she looked at me.

'Uh, yeah.'

'Good. I'll see you later.' She pecked me on the cheek and sauntered off.

I felt eyes on me and looked to see Sabiha glaring at me. I flushed.

The bell rang. Dina and Sabiha walked ahead of us while Brian stepped in with me.

'What are you doing?' he demanded.

'Nothing.'

'Really? Because it looks like you're flirting with Serena.'

'I'm not. I mean, she's flirting with me.'

Brian shook his head in disappointment. 'You're fucking this up, bro.' He walked ahead, and I followed, feeling like crap. Maybe he was right. Maybe I was fucking it up?

The rest of the day, we carefully interacted with each other under the guise of the Sassy Saints. Sabiha and I settled into a friendship again, and I vacillated between regret and relief over the next few days.

I was in the library with Charlie when Brian appeared. 'We have to talk.'

'Okay.' I lifted my eyes from the screen.

'In private.' Brian nodded at the library full of students. He headed out, and I followed him. We went to the Arts block, and in a doorway where there was no one else.

'I need to tell you about a photo of Sabiha that might circulate.'

'What?' My stomach dropped. What had happened now? Brian told me about Alma and Alex Payne dating and how he'd blackmailed her to stay together because of a sexting pic.

'So you see, Sabiha told him she'd say it was a photo of her. She had to step up and save her little sister. But it means nothing because she did nothing.'

'Okay.' I nodded dazedly, attempting to process the whole secret life that Alma had been living. I couldn't believe that Sabiha was seriously doing this and blackmailing Alex back, that she'd go to the police and tell them his nude photo was of her. I spent the last few periods in a daze, wanting to speak to Sabiha and check in with her, but we didn't share any classes.

The end-of-school bell rang, and I ran to my locker, and headed to the front. Brian caught up with me, and we found Sabiha and Alma talking. Dina was already gone for the day, as her mother had picked her up.

'Can we talk?' I asked. She nodded and followed me. 'Brian told me about what happened with Alex Payne. Are you okay?'

'I'm fine.' She kept her face neutral, but her hands gripped the backpack straps on her shoulders tightly.

'Are you sure you should do this? Maybe you need to get the police involved.'

She was shaking her head before I even finished. 'No, I have to make sure Alma is safe. I have nothing to lose. She has everything.'

I knew Alma's parents were very traditional. They'd even struggled with her having male friends. I shuddered to think how they'd react to her secret boyfriend and secret sexting scandal. 'Still, this is a lot. I mean—' I lifted my hands to encompass the school. If the photo leaked, she'd get so much negative attention.

'It's fine.' Her voice wavered as she spoke, and I realised how much it was costing her. My eyes burnt. All this time, I'd thought she was selfish and self-involved, and she could be. But she was also loyal and loving to a fault. And I'd nearly wasted my shot.

'I mean, I am that girl.' She glanced at me and quickly away.

'No, you're not. You're not at all. I'm so sorry I made you feel like that. That you weren't good enough because of what happened with Brian.' I felt like a heel. What had I done? My fear and hesitation had made her feel like she wasn't worthy when she was everything.

She stared down.

'I — I—.' I took a deep breath, working through my stuttering. 'I was wrong.' I put my hand under her chin and tilted her to look at me. 'I was scared. I've been into you for so long, so long.' My lips tilted into wry smile. 'And you never looked my way. And I just didn't believe it. I didn't believe that it was real.'

She put her hand on mine and held it against her face. 'It is. I love you, Jesse. I'm sorry it took so long for me to realise it. But it's you. It's always been you.' Sabiha stared straight into my eyes. It took me a moment to process.

'You what?' I asked, stupefied.

'I love you.'

'Oh.' I said. Was this real? There was nothing but honesty in her eyes. I allowed myself to believe it.

'I love you Jesse James,' she whispered against my lips. If this was a dream, then I never wanted to wake up. 'Please forgive me for taking so long to tell you.'

She kissed me. I closed my eyes and kissed her back, losing myself in the moment as students swarmed around us.

She lifted her lips. 'So let's make this official. Will you, Jesse James, be my boyfriend?'

I nodded dazedly. 'Good.' She kissed me on the cheek. 'Now that we've got that settled, if I ever see you flirting with any other skank, you'll be in a world of pain.' Her face darkened in anger.

Delight filled me. She was jealous. Sabiha was jealous that Serena flirted with me.

'Same goes for you,' I said. 'No flirting with anyone else.'

'There is no one else. Only you.'

I believed her.

The bell went, and she took my hand, placing it over her shoulder and hooked her fingers in my belt loop. As we walked back to our friends, I saw people side-eying me. Who would have believed that Jesse James would triumph and get his dream girl and his dream of being a published author? My hand tightened around Sabiha's shoulders.

Dina looked at us with a smile.

'About time!'

Alma smiled sadly. Her doomed romance with Alex was weighing on her.

Brian approached. 'And the world is as it should be, with my two favourite people together.' He kissed us both on the cheek, and I laughed. 'Sassy Saints forever.'

About the author

Amra Pajalić is an award-winning author, an editor and teacher who draws on her Bosnian cultural heritage to write own voices stories for young people, who like her, are searching to mediate their identity and take pride in their diverse culture. Her short story collection *The Cuckoo's Song* (Pishukin Press, 2022*)* features previously published and prize-winning stories. Her debut novel *The Good Daughter,* was published by Text Publishing in 2009 and won the 2009 Melbourne Prize for Literature's Civic Choice Award and is re-released as *Sabiha's Dilemma* (Pishukin Press, 2022).

Her memoir *Things Nobody Knows But Me* (Transit Lounge, 2019) was shortlisted for the 2020 National Biography Award. She is co-editor of the anthology *Growing up Muslim in Australia* (Allen and Unwin, 2014) which was shortlisted for the 2015 Children's Book Council of the year awards. She works as a high school teacher and is completing a PhD in Creative Writing at La Trobe University.

Amra Pajalić publishes her dark fiction using pen name A. P. Pajalic. She also publishes romance novels under pen name Mae Archer.

SIGN UP FOR AMRA'S AUTHOR NEWSLETTER

For news, giveaways, bonus material, and sneak peeks, please sign up to her newsletter below.

www.amrapajalic.com

PLEASE LEAVE A REVIEW

If you enjoyed this book and would like to show Amra your support, please consider leaving a star rating and/or review on the website you purchased the book from.

A guide for international readers

This book is set in Australia and uses British English spelling. Some spellings may differ from those used in American English.

Australia's seasons are at opposite times to those in the northern hemisphere. Summer is December–February, autumn is March–May, winter is June–August, and spring is September–November. Christmas is in summer.

In the Australian school system, primary school is for grades Kindergarten to Grade 6, and high school is for grades Year 7–12. Secondary college is a name frequently used for high school. Tertiary education after high school is either at universities and TAFE (technical and further education) institutions.

In Australia, each school year starts in late January and finishes mid-December.

The legal drinking age in Australia is 18 years old.

AUSTUDY is financial help if you're 25 or older and studying or completing an Australian apprenticeship.

Sassy Saints

Sabiha's Dilemma was my debut novel that was traditionally published under the title *The Good Daughter*. This story was inspired by my own experiences of being from a Bosnian background, growing up in the Western suburbs of Melbourne (a low socio-economic suburb) and being brought up by a mother who suffers from Bipolar.

I loved the characters that I created and kept imagining their lives beyond the pages of the book I wrote. The year after publication I wrote a follow up novel about another character, Alma, who finds out she has a half sister she never knew, Sabiha, and through Alma's story I continued Sabiha, Jesse, Brian, Dina and Adnan's stories.

When I embarked on my indie publishing career and was preparing *Sabiha's Dilemma* for release I was hit by a wave of inspiration. What if I expanded this universe and created a series where each character had their own book? This would give me the opportunity to recreate so many of the experiences that happened off-page for each of my characters and to extend their storylines.

And so the *Sassy Saints Series* was born.

Sassy Saints Series
Follow the lives of six sassy teens coming of age in St Albans, as they navigate their sexual and cultural identity and search for belonging.

These books will be an inter-connected series that can be read out of order (I'll be keeping any spoilers off the page). If you want to follow the *Sassy Saints* journey join my mailing list and stay in the loop.

Sabiha's Dilemma

Sabiha's dilemma is being the good daughter so that her mentally ill mother is accepted back into the Bosnian community.

Alma's Loyalty

When Alma finds out that she has a half sister she never knew, she is faced with competing loyalties.

Jesse's Triumph

After Jesse's debut novel is published while he's a high school student, he contends with becoming popular.

Brian's Conflict (coming 2024)

Brian's dreams of being a designer are in conflict with his father's hopes he'll join the family business as a bricklayer.

Dina's Burden (coming 2024)

Dina carries the burden of living up to her parent's expectations to make up for her brother's errant ways.

Adnan's Secret (coming 2024)

Adnan is the perfect son carrying the weight of his migrant parent's expectations, who lives a secret life.

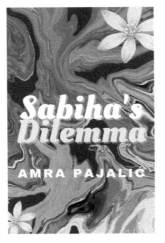

Can Sabiha play the part of the good daughter
so that her mentally ill mother is accepted back
into the Bosnian community?

Unbelievable Discounts

https://www.pishukinpress.com/

When Alma finds out that she has a half sister she never knew, she is faced with competing loyalties.

Unbelievable Discounts

https://www.pishukinpress.com/

Sabiha's Dilemma

BONUS

Jesse's Story
Sabiha and Jesse's Booklist
Adnan's Showcase Graphic
Mutusha Recipe
Songs featured

Either scan the barcode or type the hyperlink

https://www.amrapajalic.com/membersonly.html

Password: readergifts

'If you struggle to read, then you haven't found the right book format.'

I'm Amra Pajalić, the owner and publisher of Pishukin Press, an independent press dedicated to the publication of own voices fiction and nonfiction, as well as genre fiction.

There is a quote that states 'If you don't like to read, then you haven't found the right book.' I would like to extend that further and state that 'If you struggle to read then you haven't found the right book format.' As a high school teacher I have taught students with various individual needs and recognise the need to make books accessible for all kinds of readers. To this end I am committed to publishing all Pishukin Press titles in as many formats as possible. This includes:

Dyslexic Format Edition—printed in Dyslexic Open font in 14 point
Large Print edition—printed in Large Print Open Sans No Italics font in 18 point font size
Audiobooks AI—narrated by artificial intelligence using Google technology.
Audiobooks—narrated by performance narrators.
All books are also available in paperback and hardcover editions.

Learn more about Pishukin Press

https://www.pishukinpress.com/

Also by

Memoir
Things Nobody Knows But Me
Growing up Muslim in Australia

Young Adult
The Cuckoo's Song
Sabiha's Dilemma
Alma's Loyalty
Jesse's Triumph
The Climb

Romance as Mae Archer
Return to Me
Hollywood Dreams
Vintage Dreams
Dark Fiction/Horror as A.P. Pajalic
Woman on the Edge

Milton Keynes UK
Ingram Content Group UK Ltd.
UKHW040630141123
432540UK00004B/154